From the Files of

Madison Finn

Read all the books about Madison Finn!

From the Files of

Madison Finn

Thanks for Nothing

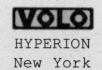

By Laura Dower

HYPERION
New York

Printed in the United States of America

First Edition
1 3 5 7 9 10 8 6 4 2

The main body of text of this book is set in 13-point Frutiger Roman.

ISBN 0-7868-1557-4

Visit www.madisonfinn.com

For Crawford with thanks for *everything*

In memory of CB and Bogie

Chapter 1

"Nooooooo!" Madison covered her face with her hands and peeked through her fingers.

This e-mail was bad news.

From: GoGramma
To: MadFinn
Subject: Thanksgiving
Date: Sat 11 Nov 7:56 AM

I am so very sorry, Maddie, but
I won't be coming to your house
for Thanksgiving. My hip problem
is back, and I'm not traveling
anywhere. Your aunt Angie is
spending the holiday with your uncle
Bob's family, so our traditional

visit is on hold until next year.
Don't be sad. I will miss you and
Phin very much. At least we can
talk online now. I finally have the
hang of this e-mail.

How did your report card go? How is
your friend Aimee? Write me another
letter.

Love, Gramma

Madison groaned as she reread the message for the third time. When Gramma Helen didn't like something, she would say, "Maddie, that is for the birds." That was exactly how Madison felt right now. Only this Thanksgiving was going to be "for the turkeys."

How could Gramma not come to Far Hills? Madison deleted the yucky message.

For the past twelve years, Madison's parents had hosted a major feast every Thanksgiving. Mom's mom, Gramma Helen, and Mom's sister, Aunt Angie, and her husband, Uncle Bob, would travel on the plane from Chicago to New York. Dad's brother, Uncle Rick, would even come from Canada with his wife, Violet, even though Canadians celebrate their Thanksgiving in October.

The Finn house had been the epicenter of everyone's Thanksgiving universe for as long as Madison could remember.

Mom always decorated the house with paper turkeys and gourds and pumpkins and spice candles. All of the town guests slept on sleeper sofas around the house—except for Gramma. Madison gave up her bedroom for Gramma. But she didn't mind. Madison loved having the house full of people . . . and so did Phin, Madison's pug. He loved all the extra attention.

Thanksgiving morning meant sleeping in, watching the Macy's parade on TV, and eating way too much good food. Dad wore an extra-large poofy white hat and called himself the house superchef. Madison was his unofficial chef-ette. She got up at five in the morning to help him make the best cornbread stuffing on the planet.

But not this year.

This year Dad wouldn't be in the Finn kitchen, thanks to the big D—D for divorce. And thanks to Gramma's bad hip and Aunt Angie and Uncle Bob's changed plans, there would be no out-of-town visitors. There wouldn't even be turkey on Madison's dinner table. Unfortunately, Mom was a vegetarian who wanted to save the turkeys, not baste them.

Madison had visions of eating a Thanksgiving bean burrito and tofu stuffing with cranberry sauce this year.

Phin was curled up in a ball on the floor, snoring, oblivious to the change in holiday plans. Would he miss the Thanksgiving attention even more than

Madison would? He'd surely miss turkey scraps tossed under the table.

"Maddie, did you call me? Do you need something?" Mom rushed upstairs and found Madison curled up on her plastic purple chair in the center of her room. "I heard you scream and . . . hey! What's that look on your face?"

Madison pouted. "Gramma can't come to Thanksgiving." She leaned over to pet Phin's ears. He made a snuffling noise.

"She e-mailed you, huh?" Mom frowned. "She said she would."

Madison could tell from Mom's tone of voice that she knew about the change in plans already.

"I'm sorry, honey bear," Mom added. "Gramma wanted to tell you herself. I know how disappointed you must—"

"Thanksgiving STINKS." Madison crossed her arms. "Can't we go to Chicago to see everyone?"

"I told you I have work commitments that week. I'm so sorry, Maddie. Really I am. Next year we can—"

"Next year?" Madison said. "What about this year?"

"This year will be just the two of us. Is that so bad?" Mom chuckled, trying to make light of the situation. But Madison wasn't laughing back.

"I knew everything would be ruined when I saw a black cat yesterday," Madison moaned. She believed that it was terrible luck for a person to walk under ladders or cross a black cat's path. Bad Thanksgiving luck had definitely found her.

"But we'll have fun together!" Mom said with a big smile. "Won't we?"

"I guess." Madison shrugged.

Mom took a deep breath.

"What's Aimee doing for Thanksgiving?"

"Having a normal day. Her family isn't divorced," Madison snapped.

The moment she'd said the words, Madison knew how hurtful they sounded. She reached for Mom's arm.

"I didn't mean that." Madison gulped. "I am so sorry, Mom."

Mom threw her arms around Madison's shoulders and squeezed. "I'm sorry, too. I know our new arrangements take some getting used to. But Angie and Bob will come next year. So will Gramma."

As Mom hugged, Madison felt all her feelings swell up inside like she would burst. But she held back from crying.

"Let's just make the best of it, okay, Maddie?" Mom said, gently smoothing the top of Madison's head.

Madison nodded. She didn't really have a choice. Whether she liked it or not, certain rules about holidays had been set up in the Finns' divorce arrangements. The judge had ruled that Mom and Dad swap Madison from holiday to holiday. This year, Mom got

Thanksgiving. Next year, Dad would.

The back-and-forth between Mom and Dad made Madison dizzier than dizzy on a regular basis. Holidays, however, were proving to be the worst. In this family tug-of-war, Madison Finn was *definitely* all pulled out.

The doorbell zinged. Madison leaped up and dashed downstairs to get the door.

Aimee was standing on the back porch, arms waving in the air, her dog Blossom's tail thwacking against the sliding doors. From inside, Phin started panting, he was so happy to see his doggy girlfriend through the glass.

"What are you doing here, Aim? I was just gonna call you!" Madison said as she opened the doors. Blossom dashed inside and ran off with Phin.

Aimee struck a pose with her hands up in the air. She was wearing a brand-new yellow winter parka.

"Whaddya think?" she asked. "I ordered it online from Boop-Dee-Doop. Well, my mother did. We ordered it on her credit card. My first Internet purchase ever."

Madison shook her head. "Cool color."

"It's called Lemon Drop," Aimee said.

"It's nice. But in case you hadn't noticed, Aimee, it's like fifty degrees outside."

Aimee pulled the jacket off. "I know. I know. But I just couldn't wait to show you. That's why I came over."

Madison decided to make it a special occasion. She took out the blender to make yellow fruit smoothies in honor of the jacket. Making smoothies was one of Madison's favorite things to do.

"Put extra banana in mine," Aimee requested.

They watched the blender go.

"I just found out my gramma isn't coming for Thanksgiving," Madison said, adding ice into the machine.

"Bummer." Aimee sighed.

"Yeah." Madison sighed back. She poured the smoothie into a glass. "So what's happening at your house for the holiday?"

Aimee shrugged and took a big slurp. "Mom is making some kind of health food dinner, as usual. My brothers begged for turkey, so we're having one of those, too. You know the drill."

"Uh-huh. The drill."

Aimee looked at Madison sideways. "Is something wrong, Maddie?"

"I wish that I had the usual drill for Thanksgiving."

"Yeah, you have to spend Thanksgiving without your dad," Aimee said. "That's stinky."

"Without my dad. Without my gramma," Madison said. "Without *everyone*. It's just gonna be Mom and me. And two people can't have a real Thanksgiving alone together."

"Why don't you guys go to Chicago?" Aimee asked.

"Mom's work." Madison sighed again. "Some project she has to do. I wish I were you or Fiona. She gets to go all the way to California for Thanksgiving."

Fiona Waters was Madison and Aimee's brand-new seventh-grade best friend. She'd moved to Far Hills from California over the summer with her twin brother, Chet.

"Fiona said her gramps has a great big swimming pool out there." Aimee giggled. "They'll be swimming on Thanksgiving! Now *that's* weird."

Aimee twirled around. She danced when she wanted to cheer her friends up, and Madison looked like she could use some cheering.

Madison cracked a smile.

"So are you gonna do that extra-credit project in social studies?" Aimee asked, waving her arms in a circle over her head.

Social studies was the one class Madison, Aimee, and Fiona had together. Their teacher, Mrs. Belden, had a reputation for being one of the toughest teachers in junior high—but she always gave kids a chance to do extra-credit projects. She said hard work was good, but it was just as important to have fun.

"I don't get why she calls it extra credit when *everyone* has to do it," Madison moaned. "And why do we all have to pair up?"

"I don't know. But we could do our project together. We can make a turkey or something."

"A turkey?" Madison exclaimed. "Like what? A turkey sandwich?"

Aimee laughed. "Sure. Let's make a mini-replica of the first Thanksgiving dinner with little drumsticks and corn on the cobs. . . ."

"Hey, what time is it?" Madison asked all of a sudden.

Outside, the sun was dipping down in the sky. It cast the entire room in an orange glow.

Aimee looked at her yellow wristwatch. She had watchbands to color-coordinate with each outfit, including her new parka. "Wow, it's almost five o'clock. Already four-thirty."

"It's getting late. Let's take the dogs out," Madison squealed. "Blossom! Phin!"

Blossom came running with Phin. They were panting like crazy.

"Wanna go OUT?" Madison said. Aimee laughed and grabbed the leashes.

It was fun to walk the dogs together. Madison and Aimee liked to think that their dogs were best friends, just like them.

When Madison returned home, Mom was perched on the sofa, watching edited reels from one of her documentary films.

"I'm going up to my room," Madison announced.

Mom didn't flinch.

"I'm going up to my room," Madison announced again, louder this time.

"Okay. Dinner's in an hour," Mom said, waving her off. "And clean that mess. And finish your homework."

Madison made a face, only Mom didn't see it. Mom sounded like a recorded message: do this, clean that.

Once upstairs, Madison consciously decided not to pick *anything* up. She crawled over her enormous pile of clothes and pile of files and collapsed into her purple chair. There were much better things to do than clean her room! She powered up her laptop.

Madison had only intended to log on, send an e-mail back to Gramma, and log off. But once online, she got *way* distracted from those tasks. She surfed around and went to the home page for bigfishbowl.com. There was a new feature advertised on a flashing yellow banner across the top.

Just Fishing Around! The Ultimate Search Engine!

Madison typed in the word *dog* for fun, just to see what a search on her favorite subject might turn up. Madison was pleasantly surprised to see 3,412 possible matches and started reading. Links were underlined.

<u>**Dog** Owner's Guide: Welcome to **Dog**</u>
<u>Owner's Guide</u>
If you have a **dog**, want a **dog**, or love **dog**s, you've come to the right place for all kinds of information

about living with and loving **dog**s.
Includes **Dog** Screen Saver, more.

Dog Emporium Online
Flea collars, heartworm pills, soft
beds, chew toys, rawhide . . .
everything discounted for your
family **dog**.

Dog of the Day—Sign Yours Up Now
Tell us about your special **dog**. Is
your bichon frise funny? Does your
weimaraner whine? Winners daily!

Madison added a few more words to the search
to find dog links closer to home. She typed in DOG,
FAR HILLS, NEW YORK—separated by the required
commas. A familiar name popped up.
Madison knew this vet!

Far Hills Animal Shelter, Clinic,
Dog Boarding
Welcome from Bryan Wing, DVM, and
staff. Full service, referrals, **dog**
boarding, Tales of Homeless Pets,
Breed Tips, **dog** grooming care.
Volunteers needed!

Dr. Wing was married to Madison's computer
teacher, Mrs. Wing. This was the direct link for Dr.
Wing's Web site.
On the site's home page there was a photograph

of a basset hound that looked just like Aimee's dog, Blossom. That dissolved slowly into a photo of a yellow Labrador retriever (who was really more cream colored than yellow) and a teeny dachshund named Rosebud. More flashing type at the bottom of the screen read: *Come and visit our offices!* There was a teeny photograph of Dr. Wing and a short letter underneath that.

Welcome to Far Hills Animal Shelter and Clinic! We're glad you've stopped into the section of our "virtual" animal shelter. For ten years, my team has been dedicated to pet rescue and care in Far Hills. Working with shelters, veterinarians, and other concerned businesses, we hope to eliminate our homeless pet problem and care for sick and abandoned animals in our area. Won't you please become a volunteer and help out?

"Rooooowowf!" Phin barked. He was curled up into a ball by the base of Madison's purple chair. Madison scratched Phin's head.

The idea of helping out at the animal shelter seemed so exciting. Maybe this year's Thanksgiving didn't have to be for the turkeys after all? Maybe this Thanksgiving could be for the *dogs* instead?

Phin would *definitely* love that.

Chapter 2

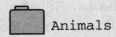 Animals

Mom thinks I should still be taking flute lessons, but I am soooo over the musical instrument thing. I am going to be an animal volunteer. That makes more sense, since I have loved animals my entire life.

Here is a list of all the pets that I have had:

1. Sea monkeys in a plastic jar.
2. Goldfish named Peanut Butter and Jelly because one was yellow and the other was sort of purple.
3. Ick, my cat. I named him that because he threw up fur balls a lot.
4. Phinnie, the best dog ever. I love my pug better than any pet!

My biggest wish in life would be to live on a farm or near a zoo or in the apartment over Wink's pet shop in Far Hills so I could see more animals all the time and Phin would have more animals to play with. I wonder what the shelter will be like? Dr. Wing's Web site says they take care of sick animals and do "animal rescue." I wonder if that's some kind of animal SWAT team?

Rude Awakening: It's a dog-meet-dog world and I want to be part of it RIGHT NOW.

"What a wonderful idea, Maddie," Mom said when Madison told her about the Far Hills Animal Shelter. "I'm happy that you want to volunteer—especially at Thanksgiving time. And it's only a short ride over there. We can drive over today to check it out."

As Mom drove them to the clinic downtown, Madison could feel her entire body humming. *Would the animals at the clinic like her? Would she like the animals? What would Dr. Wing say when he saw her?*

Madison fussed and twisted in the car's front seat. The belt felt so snug. She couldn't stay still. This ride was taking forever!

"Well, there's the clinic," Mom announced. "At last!"

She pointed to a squat-looking, pink cement

building with an iron gate and planters filled with mums out front. A teeny neon sign blinked HOSPITAL under a bigger, painted, wood sign that bore the clinic's name: FAR HILLS ANIMAL SHELTER.

"Maddie, are you going to just sit there or are we going inside?" Mom teased. Madison led the way as they got out of the car.

"It looks nice from the outside, right, Mom?" Madison said as she approached the clinic slowly. Each stepping-stone was shaped like a dog bone.

"Doggies everywhere," Mom said, pointing out photos of different dog breeds on a poster in the clinic window. "Phin sure would be jealous."

"Hiya!" chirped a blond woman wearing a white lab coat and a purple T-shirt. The shirt read I'M FOR FUR-FREE. She introduced herself as Eileen and stood behind the front desk like she guarded the place.

"Hi," Madison said. "I'm looking for Dr. Wing—"

"Pet problems?" Eileen interrupted. "Well, we can help you. We got all sorts of pets here. In all shapes and sizes."

"We're not looking for a pet or bringing in a pet," Mom said. "My daughter would like to volunteer. She goes to Far Hills Junior High, and she says she saw your Web—"

"Volunteer? Well, sure!" Eileen said. "Why don't you have a seat and I can help you both in just a sec." She stepped into a back room.

The front door of the clinic opened with a gust of

air, and a bearded bald man came inside with a parrot on his shoulder. He took a seat by the door across from a woman who was holding an empty leash. Madison saw little animal hairs all over the woman's clothes.

Pets always leave their mark on people, Madison thought. She looked down at the chew marks at the edge of her own sneaker.

"Heeere's Gidget!" Eileen reappeared in the waiting room holding a teeny, yipping white dog. The animal made a jump for its owner, trembling and shedding more onto her black sweater.

"Come here, Gidgie-widgie, come here," the owner cooed. The white dog looked happier than happy.

Next Eileen turned to the bearded man. "So, Mr. Walsh, it looks like Rose is losing some feathers again."

Eileen stroked the top of the parrot's head, and it nipped at her fingers. But she didn't seem to mind.

"Rosie is losing as many feathers as I'm losing hair," the old man said. "And I swear I've been feeding her that special seed you told me about."

Rose squawked as Eileen took her back into the examining room. "We'll have you all fixed up in a jiffy, Rosie. Not to worry. And you shouldn't worry, either, Mr. Walsh."

Madison wondered what was behind the door that everyone seemed to disappear behind. As usual, questions streamed into her mind like floodwater.

Were there several different kinds of examining rooms?

Did the clinic have an operating room, too?

Where did the animals live and stay?

Were there cages and fish tanks and fenced-in pens?

And where was Dr. Wing?

Madison stood up and craned her neck to see if she could catch a look in back. Eileen was taking longer than she said.

Meanwhile Mom was hardly noticing any of the dog or parrot activity in the waiting room. Ever since she'd begun development of her latest film project, she did work every chance she got—even in the middle of a veterinarian's waiting room. She was busy checking work messages on her cell phone.

Madison counted red linoleum squares on the floor. She could see where dog paws and cat pads and other pet footprints had left their mark.

Eileen returned in a flurry. "So, here are the forms to fill out," she said.

Being only twelve, Madison needed special parental permission to volunteer. Mom adjusted her cell phone on her ear and scanned the forms for a place to sign. She put her name on the line under Madison's own signature.

Finally Madison handed the pages to Eileen. "Are you a doctor too, like Dr. Wing?" Madison asked.

Eileen winked. "More like an animal nurse. I help Dr. Wing with almost everything. And I run this place on weekends. We're open mostly for emergencies and walk-ins."

"If I volunteer, will I be helping you with animal rescue?" Madison asked.

"Oh," Eileen gasped. "You'll be helping in all sorts of ways around here."

Eileen glanced over the pages to make sure everything was signed. Suddenly she looked up and smiled. "Well, I'll be. You're Madison. Madison Finn?"

"Yeah." Madison smiled nervously. She thought something was filled out wrong. Why was Eileen saying her name that way?

"From Far Hills Junior High—you said that, didn't you? I get the connection." Eileen slapped her forehead. "You see, my son is also—"

Suddenly a boy walked into the waiting room.

"Madison?"

"Dan?" Madison wrinkled her brow. It was Dan Ginsburg from school. He hung around with Madison's guy friends, Egg Diaz, Drew Maxwell, Chet Waters, and even Hart Jones. Dan was the guy who ate everyone's dessert at lunch when they didn't want it. In fifth grade, all the kids in middle school called him Pork-O, but they stopped doing it when he got way bigger than them. He was taller and wider than anyone in seventh grade.

"It is you!" Dan said, supersurprised. "No way!"

"So you two know each other?" Eileen smiled.

"Your son helps out here, too. Well, isn't that nice," Mom said, tucking her cell phone away. She seemed relieved to know that Madison wouldn't be the only twelve-year-old being a veterinarian's helper. Dan extended his hand to shake Mom's.

"Hi, Mrs. Finn," Dan said.

"This boy's a regular Dr. Dolittle, if you ask me," Eileen said.

Dan looked mortified. "Ma, do you have to—"

"Dan, I didn't know you liked animals," Madison said. "I mean, that's so cool. I love animals more than—how come you never said anything?"

"I don't know." Dan seemed flustered. "I never thought about it. I've been coming here since I was little."

"Cool," Madison said. She was genuinely impressed.

After a few more words about forms and schedules, arrangements were made for Madison to officially come back and help out at the clinic Tuesday after school. Dan said he'd be there, too.

Madison and Mom thanked Eileen and said good-bye. The door jingled as they exited, and Madison grinned to herself at the bell's tinkling. It was like a joyful ringing to mark the beginning of this new adventure. She'd be helping animals as often as she could.

Suddenly she felt less jumpy. Not only was she a real volunteer, but she even knew someone who already worked here. She couldn't wait to tell everyone. Dad would be prouder than proud. And Aimee and Fiona would think the clinic was really cool.

On the way home, Mom stopped to pick up pizza dinner. Mom was famous for picking up takeout. Tonight Madison wouldn't have to add to her Scary Dinner file. Sometimes when Mom felt like cooking, it was more than scary.

"Well, I guess you were right, Maddie. Maybe volunteering does beat flute lessons," Mom said on the car ride home. "You have a great smile on your face! I wish I had a camera. And Dan seems very nice. Wasn't he the Lion in *The Wiz*?"

Madison flashed a grin and nodded.

"Who knows, Maddie?" Mom added. "Maybe you're destined to be a vet yourself someday."

"Well," Madison mused, "I could be a vet . . . or I could be a computer programmer . . . or maybe a writer. I know I want to be famous, that's a definite."

"You'll be a vet on some weekday afternoons, anyway," Mom said, turning into their driveway. "Right now, I'd like you to take Phin for a walk. Okay?"

"Okay!" Madison hopped out of the car and skipped up the front porch steps.

"WOOOOOOOOOORRRRF!" Phin snorted a combination hello and sneeze as Madison came inside.

The dog jumped up and sniffed Madison's hands and legs and jacket and sneakers.

"Phinnie!" Madison said, leaning down to greet him. "What are you doing?"

Phin smelled something. He smelled *everything*. Was it the pizza they'd picked up on the way home? Or the Far Hills Animal Shelter all over Madison's clothes and skin? He licked her legs all over.

"Run!" Madison squealed, making a dash for the kitchen. After much petting and a handful of dog treats, Phin finally calmed down enough to go for his walk. They made their usual loop around Blueberry Street before dinner.

Madison ate a giant slice of pizza and then headed straight for her bedroom. It was getting late, and she still had science reading and math home- work. She also needed to send an e-mail to Bigwheels, her online keypal.

As she logged on to bigfishbowl.com, Madison was still wired with excitement from her trip to the Far Hills Animal Shelter.

From: MadFinn
To: Bigwheels
Subject: BIG NEWS for Bigwheels
Date: Sun 12 Nov 5:23 PM

Do you like animals? Do you have a pet? I know I asked you that but I forget. I am bouncing off the walla-wallas because my mom says I can volunteer at this animal clinic in our town. Have you ever volunteered for anything? I can't concentrate and I have to study, too. Where r u?

Please write back soon.

Yours till the puppy loves,

MadFinn

P.S. Attached is a picture of my dog, by the way. His name is Phin and he's a pug. Isn't he cute?
<<Attachment: PHINNIE.jpg>>

Just as Madison was about to log offline again, Aimee sent her an Insta-Message.

<BalletGrl>: hey I tried calling you
<MadFinn>: mom is on the line with
    clients
<BalletGrl>: how wuz the vet
<MadFinn>: sooo many 3:]
<BalletGrl>: huh
<MadFinn>: DOGS
<BalletGrl>: I get it. Meet me B4
    school tomorrow
<MadFinn>: xtra credit in SS???

```
<BalletGrl>: TOTALLY C U
<MadFinn>: woof!
<BalletGrl>: *poof*
```

Tomorrow was back to school, but Madison couldn't get her mind off the animal shelter. She'd rather spend time with dogs than Pilgrims. Maybe she and Aimee could combine the two?

Suddenly she got a silly idea.

Maybe they could do an extra-credit report on dogs that crossed on the Mayflower?

Dad would have a good laugh at that one.

Chapter 3

Monday morning Madison went to the school lobby to put her canned tomatoes in the large donation box. Egg and Fiona had just done the same thing.

"There must be five cans of yellow waxed beans in there," Egg said.

Madison laughed. "And a can of pinto beans, too. What are those?"

"It's like a vegetable graveyard," Fiona said.

Students and teachers were asked to bring canned food from home just before Thanksgiving. The cans would be given to the homeless and other needy people in the Far Hills community.

"GOOD MORNING, STUDENTS," a voice suddenly boomed from the loudspeaker, which just happened to be on the wall near Egg's head. Egg faked a sudden eardrum injury. Madison and Fiona chuckled.

"STUDENT COUNCIL MEETINGS WILL BE HELD THIS AFTERNOON IN THE ASSEMBLY," Principal Bernard said. "AND YOUR ESTEEMED CLASS PRESIDENTS WILL BE TAKING THE NAMES OF VOLUNTEERS FOR OUR ANNUAL TURKEY TROT AT THESE MEETINGS . . . AND PLEASE DON'T FORGET THE CAN DROP IN THE LOBBY. . . ."

November was a busier-than-busy month at school. While the can drive was about helping the homeless, the Turkey Trot was a short running race for students to raise money for the Far Hills Senior Center. Everywhere kids went, someone at school wanted them to give time, give cans, or give thanks.

"Why don't they just give it a rest?" Egg snapped. "Like we don't have enough to do."

"Did Principal Bernard say 'esteemed' class president? That's a joke." Fiona snickered. "Since Ivy was elected, I don't think she's done much of anything."

Madison just shrugged. Ivy Daly was their enemy number one, appropriately nicknamed Poison Ivy, but Madison wasn't in the mood to talk about her. Madison had more important things on her mind.

"Hey, Finnster!" a voice called from across the lobby. Madison turned to say hello. She knew it was Hart Jones. He'd nicknamed her Finnster years ago and it stuck. She didn't like it very much, but somehow the way Hart said it made it seem beautiful. She was crushing on Hart big time, so when she did greet him, Madison did it very carefully.

"Oh . . . hey . . ." she said, tossing her head as casually as she could. Whenever she saw Hart's brown tousled hair and wide smile, Madison could feel her own heart thumping inside her chest.

"What's going on?" Hart asked.

Madison pretended to look for a book in her orange book bag. "Just going to class. What about you?"

DUH! Madison wanted to run as soon as she had asked that dopey question. Of course he was going to class. Where else would Hart be headed in *school*?

Egg interrupted them with a hard tug on Hart's shirt. "Hey, man, I gotta show you something. Let's go."

"See you later, Finnster," Hart said, letting himself be dragged away.

Egg and Hart had become fast friends along with Drew and Chet. They liked to travel in a pack.

"I totally love your outfit, Maddie. Did I say that already?" Fiona giggled. Madison was wearing a denim skirt and a purple T-shirt with little flowers embroidered around the neckline.

"Thanks," Madison replied. "I like your shirt, too."

"Where's Aimee?" Fiona asked.

"Probably dancing," Madison said.

Aimee sometimes took ballet private lessons in the morning before school. She was determined to be a ballerina or some kind of professional dancer when she got older, so she went to private lessons in addition to her afternoon practices for Dance Troupe. Sometimes Aimee would have to get late passes to morning classes if her ballet lessons interfered. She often made dance her number-one priority.

As the first round of bells rang, Madison said good-bye to Fiona and went to Mrs. Wing's classroom. Egg and Drew weren't there yet.

"Madison!" Mrs. Wing said, smiling from ear to ear. "My husband told me you'll be volunteering at the Far Hills clinic. I think that's terrific."

Madison felt herself blush a little bit. "He told you? But he wasn't even there when I visited."

"He goes in late on Sundays to prepare for the coming week. He saw your name on the sign-up sheets." Mrs. Wing leaned down closer to Madison. "That's a very fine thing you're doing, you know. The animals need so much attention. Good for you!"

Madison blushed a little bit more at the compliments.

Brrrrrrrring.

As the second round of bells clanged, Egg and Drew appeared suddenly at the classroom door and scurried over to two empty seats near Madison.

Egg leaned over to Drew and whispered, "Whoa. Mrs. Wing looks pretty today."

Madison couldn't believe Egg had developed a crush on Mrs. Wing when seventh grade began— and that it still hadn't fizzled. He couldn't get the goofy stare off his face whenever he was inside her classroom.

"Today we'll be learning the basics of PowerPoint programs," Mrs. Wing said. "Who can tell me what that is?"

The class was noisy, so she clapped to get everyone's attention. The satin scarf over Mrs. Wing's shoulders made a soft swoosh with each clap. The painted scarf, with autumn leaves in brown, orange, and yellow, sounded like a rustle of *real* leaves.

Egg was right, Madison thought, staring at the scarf. Mrs. Wing was so pretty. She even had a cool husband. She had a perfect life. *Perfect.*

Madison wished her family were close to perfect like that.

By the time social studies rolled around in the afternoon, Madison was all ready with a tentative outline for her extra assignment with Aimee. They had planned it out during lunch, and they were both really excited.

Unfortunately, Mrs. Belden, their social studies teacher, wasn't as enthusiastic. She had a cough and a cold and was crankier than cranky.

Rat-a-tat-a-tat-a-tat.

Mrs. Belden tapped the edge of her desk with a plastic ruler to get everyone's attention.

"As you know, I'm proposing extra-credit projects with a holiday theme."

A wave of whispers flooded the room as Mrs.

Belden pulled down a map of the original thirteen colonies and pointed to Massachusetts.

"This is Plimoth," she said. "P-l-i-m-o-t-h, as they spelled it back then."

Egg and Drew were chattering. Madison felt certain they'd agreed in advance to be partners.

Fiona was across the room talking to her soccer buddy, Daisy. The circle of friends had agreed ahead of time that if Madison and Aimee partnered, Fiona and Daisy would do the same. That way no one would feel left out.

Madison glanced around the room, to see who else might pair off together. She guessed that Ivy and one of her drones would be partners. Rose Thorn and Phony Joanie were always right by Ivy's side.

Mrs. Belden kept talking over all the distractions and noise. "Class! Now listen up. I want you to do these projects in pairs. I think that if we can work together better as a group, we may begin to have a little more discipline about our work. You all have loads of great ideas, so it should be fun working together."

Hart raised his hand. "So can we pick our extra-credit partners?" he asked.

Aimee and Madison looked at each other with a smile, and then Mrs. Belden shook her head no.

Madison's stomach did a 180-degree flip-flop. Aimee's hand shot into the air.

Mrs. Belden kept right on talking.

"Actually, Hart, the topic of your project will be up to you, but pairs working together will be chosen by me. This isn't really a voluntary thing, either. I've decided everyone must do the extra credit. And yes, that includes you, Ben."

Ben Buckley, the smartest kid in the room and probably in the entire school, didn't look happy with that news.

Madison's jaw dropped. She scribbled in the margin of her notebook: MAYBE U WILL STILL BE MY PARTNER?

Aimee wrote in the margin of her notebook: HOPE SO.

Mrs. Belden read from a list of names and pointed to different student pairs-to-be. Fiona and Daisy were matched up first. Madison felt more hopeful that Aimee would be her partner.

Next Ivy was matched up with Drew. Everyone giggled out loud. The thought of a boy-and-girl pair—especially *that* pair—was so funny. Drew looked especially embarrassed. Poison Ivy looked . . . well, disgusted. Then again, Madison always thought she looked that way.

"Hart Jones and Dan Ginsburg." Mrs. Belden read the next pair off her list. The two boys smiled and high-fived on the other side of the room.

Madison kept up hope that she and Aimee would be paired.

"Madison Finn." Mrs. Belden read her name off the list, and Madison took a huge breath. "Your partner will be . . ."

Madison listened closer than close.

". . . Walter Diaz," Mrs. Belden said.

Madison gulped. *Egg?* She'd been matched up with her closest guy friend? Was that a bad thing or a good thing? She couldn't decide.

Aimee punched Madison on the shoulder. "You're soooo lucky," Aimee whispered. "Now who am I gonna get?"

The answer came a moment later.

"Aimee Gillespie, I'd like you to work with Ben Buckley."

Aimee tried not to look appalled. Madison knew she was. Ben was *way* obnoxious. With his super-snobby attitude, he would have been a much better partner for Poison Ivy.

"I'm so bummed," Madison moaned as soon as class had ended. She and Fiona and Aimee went to their lockers. "I'm bummed that we won't be partners, Aim."

"Well, Ben may be superstrange, but at least he's supersmart, too," Aimee said. "That'll make up for his personality, won't it?"

"All that really and truly matters is that we didn't get the Princess of Evil," Madison whispered, motioning to Ivy, who just happened to be walking past at that very moment. The three friends stared.

"Uh, can I help you?" Ivy snarled, nose in the air. She made a face and walked on by with Rose Thorn and Phony Joanie.

"Maddie!" Egg yelled. He ran up to the girls. "How cool is this? We got matched. I have a great idea already. You are gonna be so glad you got me."

Madison wasn't surprised that Egg acted a little full of himself. She knew he would want to be the one in charge. "I have things totally under control," he said.

"You do?" Madison asked. "But we haven't even decided what we're doing."

Aimee rolled her eyes. "You're like . . . a total turkey, Egg."

"But turkey's okay, since it is Thanksgiving," Madison said, grinning.

Egg laughed. "Very funny, Maddie. Just hilarious," he said.

As they packed up their bags to head home, Madison tried to adjust her outlook on the entire situation. "I think we'll be great," Madison said.

Egg pushed her shoulder. "Hey, I'll e-mail you later, okay?" He ran off to find Chet.

Madison noticed Fiona staring at Egg when he disappeared around the corner. Everyone knew Fiona had a mega-crush on him. Madison wondered if maybe Egg liked Fiona more than he admitted, too.

Later that afternoon, Madison went online to find ideas for her extra-credit project with Egg. She checked her e-mailbox and was surprised to find it full of messages.

FROM	SUBJECT
✉ Boop-Dee-Doop	special offers
✉ Bigfishbowl	SANDWICH POLL
✉ JeffFinn	ANOTHER JOKE!!
✉ FHC	Welcome!

Boop-Dee-Doop announced 10 percent off all merchandise, which was great news, since Madison was saving up her allowance for a pair of flared jeans with a low waist and patches on the back.

Bigfishbowl.com was announcing the results of their Sandwich Day poll. They always celebrated obscure holidays that no one ever really heard of. Sandwich Day was November 3. The yummiest sandwich according to the bigfishbowl.com poll takers was peanut butter and jelly. Hamburgers came in a close second.

Next Madison read the e-mail from JeffFinn, aka Dad. Madison knew that he would probably send her at least one joke a day until Thanksgiving.

From: JeffFinn
To: MadFinn
Subject: ANOTHER JOKE!!
Date: Mon 13 Nov 4:23 PM

If April showers bring May flowers, what do May flowers bring?

```
Guess this and I'll take you to
dinner.

I love you,

Dad
```

Madison groaned. Didn't Dad realize he'd been telling her that same joke since she was four years old? The answer was "Pilgrims," of course.
Duh!

She was about to click DELETE but stopped herself. Dad hadn't mentioned anything in his note about Thanksgiving dinner. She reread it.

Madison secretly wished that Dad would protest all the divorce rules so they could all have a big old turkey dinner together. But Dad never protested much of anything.

The only e-mail remaining took Madison by surprise. The Far Hills Clinic (FHC) had sent Madison a welcome letter.

```
From: FHC
To: MadFinn
Subject: Welcome!
Date: Mon 13 Nov 4:08 PM
```
Woof! We're so happy to welcome
you, Madison Finn, to our Far Hills
family of volunteers. Thanks to
people like you, we can provide

care and help for animals in our community. That's something to bark about! We look forward to seeing you on your first day. If you have not signed up yet, please call Eileen Ginsburg at the clinic—she'll be pleased to put you on our schedule.

Thank you,

Dr. Bryan Wing
and all the animals at FHC

Although the family parts of Thanksgiving between Mom and Dad still needed a little sorting out, the school parts seemed to be working out well—and this e-mail indicated that the volunteering would be good fun, too. Gramma Helen would say, "Don't count your turkeys before they're hatched."

But these days, Madison Finn wanted to count on *everything*.

Chapter 4

"Well, hiya!" Eileen said when Madison walked into the clinic on the next day. "Are you ready to work?"

Madison could feel her face flush. *Ready?* She was readier than ready to meet and help each and every animal.

Eileen showed her to a back room where the cages were kept. Barks, squawks, growls, and whines came from every direction. There were mostly dogs doing all the talking, but Madison spotted a few other critters and birds who had something to say. A tabby cat was curled up in the corner of one cage with a cast on his leg. He couldn't stop meowing.

"Poor Freddie. Wounded in a cat fight," Eileen said, stroking Fred's ears through the cage door. "He's under a little medication. That's why his eyes are all glassy and he's so talkative. We'll keep him sedated for a day or two until he has a chance to start healing."

Eileen introduced Madison to other staff members and showed her around the clinic. Madison learned that the clinic "emergency room" was where the veterinarian on call would help an animal recover until its wounds healed. Like right now. Sometimes the animal brought in would be a family pet. But most of the time, the clinic dealt with strays and unwanted animals from the community.

Madison felt sad when she discovered just how many different animals were abandoned in Far Hills—even sweet cats like Fred.

Dr. Wing stepped into the room. He smiled at Madison and went over to the cage where the yellow Labrador retriever named Spanky lay awake, but breathing heavily. The dog had an anxiety disorder, so the doctor had given him a sedative to calm his nerves.

"Hey, Dr. Wing," Madison said when he looked up. He looked a little different from the last time Madison had seen him, at the seventh-grade dance. There he had been wearing a costume.

"Hi, Madison," Dr. Wing said. "Have you met the other volunteers?"

"Other volunteers?" Madison repeated. Was there a whole crowd of people squished together in the back?

"We have a lot of people doing different duties around here. You'll meet them all at some point," Dr. Wing explained.

Eileen pressed against the small of Madison's back and pushed her gently. "Next stop, kennel room. Here we go, Madison."

Madison's five senses were overwhelmed once again as they passed into the new area. A woman with a red beehive hairdo and a lab coat with a tag that read STAFF smiled. The air smelled like wet dog.

As they passed into the place Eileen called the kennel, Madison eyed medicine cabinets crammed with jars and bottles, Technicolor posters of animal anatomy, a bulletin board covered with Polaroid photographs of posed pets, and overflowing barrels of kibble. It was impossible to see, smell, or hear everything at once.

Half the cages were filled with dogs in assorted shapes and sizes. Some had scars on their fur and skin. Some were fast asleep, others just scared. Many barked at the slightest human movement. A home-made sign over the row of cages read DOG POUND—TAKE ME HOME!

Dan was in the corner with an older man he called Mr. Wollensky.

Mr. Wollensky smiled. "Have you met our fam-il-eee?" he asked with a thick Russian accent. The dogs howled as he spritzed the hose around their cages.

"Madison, help me move some of these dogs. We have to wash out their cages," Dan said, opening a cage door. A wirehaired dog was huddled, shaking, in a corner.

"Awww, she's so cute," Madison said, biting her lip as she tentatively moved toward the cage. She let the dog sniff her hand first, since she didn't know if these dogs were friendly or not.

"Hello, Pepper." Dan laughed. "Dr. Wing lets me name puppies sometimes when they come in nameless. I named her that because she made me sneeze." Dan petted her head. "You can take Pepper out if you want."

"Awww." Madison smiled at the pup. "Don't be scared." She helped lift Pepper out of the cage and into a small pen to play with rubber chew toys until her cage was washed out.

Mr. Wollensky sprayed the hose more, and Madison got a little wet. It was fun to be helping out immediately after she arrived.

"Eileen?" Dr. Wing poked his head into the back room. "Dan, have you seen your mother? I need her help."

Dan dashed off to find his mother. Madison wondered if Dan got to sit in on the medical examinations. He'd been working at the Far Hills Animal Shelter and Clinic since he was five. Madison had only been here for five minutes.

Madison reached down and picked up Pepper, who licked her face. "You're a cutie pie, Pep."

"Yip!" Pepper said, as if she understood.

While Mr. Wollensky continued to hose down the dog area, Madison helped transfer other dogs one by one into the waiting pen and then back into their cages. She read signs on their cages that listed their names, date of arrival, and medical condition if any.

Blinky, arrived October 15, abandoned, eye infection.

Blinky looked like he was crying nonstop, which Madison assumed accounted for his name. He lay there like a sack, breathing deep, paws crossed. Madison looked real close to make sure he was alive.

"That is sickie dog," Mr. Wollensky said.

"Huh? What kind of dog is Blinky?" Madison asked.

He leaned in and adjusted his hearing aid. "I say sickie dog. Yes?"

Madison had trouble understanding Mr. Wollensky. His hearing problem and Russian accent made it hard to communicate with him. But he was very gentle. Mr. Wollensky seemed to love animals as much as Madison did.

Mr. Wollensky reached out for Madison's arm. "You no touch these dog," he cautioned her. "Bad dog."

Pavlov, arrived September 30, neglected. Handle with care. Bites.

Pavlov growled from behind the bars. Mr. Wollensky explained in broken English about how he'd named this particular dog Pavlov after a *Russian* doctor who conducted special kinds of science experiments. Dr. Pavlov was a man who tested whether a ringing a bell could trigger a hunger response in his dog. It worked. Since then, conditioned responses were called Pavlovian responses.

Madison could barely understand what else Mr. Wollensky was saying, but she decided he was very nice. He introduced Madison to the remaining animals in cages, including a cat named Whisky that was going bald, a bulldog that was waiting to be spayed, and a hyperactive puppy named Kazoo.

"No become too attached," Mr. Wollensky said. "Then you be sad when dog go."

Madison told him getting attached wouldn't be a problem.

"I already have a dog," she explained to Mr. Wollensky. He just smiled and nodded and smiled. Madison figured he didn't understand a word she was saying.

The clock on the kennel-room wall said it was almost time to head home, so Madison used the office phone to call Mom for her ride.

Mom wasn't really talkative on the way home or even during dinner—take-out Chinese. She asked Madison to help fold laundry down in the basement, so they went downstairs together.

"Tell me again about the cute dogs," Mom said after a few rounds of fold-the-bedsheets-and-towels.

Madison perked up. "Mom, I think volunteering was the smartest thing I've ever done. Ever."

Mom sighed. "You do a lot of smart things, honey bear."

Phinnie came clinking down the stairs. Madison and Mom turned to look at him. As he reached the bottom, he sat there a little lopsided, tongue hanging out, snorting like mad.

Mom sighed again. "Oh, I wish Thanksgiving could be different this year, sweetheart, I really do."

"We—we don't have to talk about that," Madison stammered. "You seem sad."

"The whole arrangement has been on my mind since Sunday. You seemed so disappointed with it just being us two for dinner," Mom said. "I didn't know what to say to you. I feel bad about it."

Madison couldn't believe her mom was being so honest.

"I'm so NOT disappointed, Mom," Madison said, lying through her teeth.

Mom shrugged. "Well . . . to tell you the truth, Maddie, I am. I'm a little disappointed. I miss the family the way it was. I miss my family."

Together, in silence, they folded one last fitted sheet, and then Madison went upstairs to go to sleep. Before she changed into her pajamas, Madison booted up her computer for an e-mail check, quietly so Mom wouldn't hear.

Two e-mails flashed. Both came from real friends.

The first one distracted Madison a little from everything Mom had been talking about. It was from Egg, and his spelling was as bad as ever.

From: Eggaway
To: MadFinn
Subject: CLASS PROJECT
Date: Tues 7 Nov 7:31 PM

I have been thinkin about the project Mrs. Belden & thinkweshould do something about pligrims maybe. Like build a model. I found cool Websits that have infoand pictures. What do u think? LMK. Bye!!!

Bigwheels got in touch, too. Madison was so relieved.

From: Bigwheels
To: MadFinn
Subject: Gobble gobble
Date: Tues 14 Nov 9:18 PM

You are way better at writing than me. The answer to your question is YES about Thanksgiving. We have sooooo many peeps for dinner. We live in a small house, so Mom and Dad and my aunts and uncles and us kids rent a hotel space for dinner. It is so weird. I think that last yr. there were like 86 of us. I didn't even know them all and I'm related to them!!! My sisters were freaked, too. It makes you claustrophobic (did I spell that right?)

Don't worry about your Thanksgiving because it will work out no matter where you are. We should be super thankful, right? You don't need lots of people. Besides you have ME!!!

Yours till the turkey gobbles,

Bigwheels

p.s. Tell more about the animal shelter in ur next e-mail

Bigwheels was right. Madison closed her laptop and decided right then and there that she had to stop worrying about being alone with Mom on Thanksgiving. She had to stop worrying, period. The divorce had happened, and there was nothing to be done about it. No matter how hard she wished, nothing could bring Dad and Mom back together.

Madison suddenly thought about all the animals in the shelter, woofing and sniffling and giving her kisses. They seemed so lost and needy without their own families. Madison wondered: if she couldn't change things with Mom and Dad, maybe she could help the animals instead?

Closing her eyes to sleep, Madison's whole body warmed to the idea. She drifted to sleep counting . . . not sheep, but puppies.

Puppies and puppies and more puppies . . .

Chapter 5

Between fourth and fifth period Madison met Aimee and Fiona in the second-floor girls' bathroom. Since they didn't always have class together, they'd try to steal some time in between classes, away from teachers and everyone else. They liked sneaking even just a few minutes of gossip and giggles.

Today Fiona was complaining a little about her social studies partner, Daisy Espinoza.

"She's amazing at soccer," Fiona said. "But she's really not very good at this whole project thing."

Aimee shrugged and leaned into the bathroom mirror. Madison watched her intently. Aimee was touching up her lip gloss.

"What do you guys think?" Fiona asked. "Should I ask to switch partners?"

"I don't think you can," Madison moaned.

"Otherwise I would have done it already."

"That's not true," Aimee said all of a sudden. "You got Egg as a partner. He's a good match."

"Yeah, well . . ." Madison shrugged.

"Egg is soooo cute," Fiona grinned. "I mean . . . well, you know what I mean. . . ." She looked embarrassed all of a sudden.

"Yeah, whatever you say, Fiona." Madison laughed a little because she knew all about Fiona's supercrush. Fiona acted so goofy whenever Egg's name was even mentioned.

Madison hopped up to sit on the radiator next to the sinks. Thankfully, the heat wasn't turned on full. A bell went off. They had three minutes before the next class period.

Aimee pinched her cheeks to make them pinker. She didn't take her eyes off her reflection.

"Do you guys think Ben Buckley is cute?" Aimee asked softly.

Madison covered her mouth so she wouldn't gasp with laughter, but she started to giggle.

Fiona bit her lip. "Are you serious?"

Aimee swirled around and asked her friends, "Why are you looking at me like that? Okay, I know Ben's obnoxious, but . . ."

Before she could say another word, the bathroom door was flung open. Poison Ivy Daly and her drones buzzed inside. But Ivy stopped short when she saw Madison, Aimee, and Fiona.

By now, Madison was giggling *out loud*. Ivy was taken aback.

"Oh, I didn't know this bathroom was dirty," Ivy snarled, and turned on one heel as she led the way out the door.

"What's *that* supposed to mean?" Fiona said, acting a little spacey.

Madison made a face and stuck out her tongue behind Ivy's back.

"When are you leaving for California, Fiona?" Aimee asked, as if the interruption had never happened.

Fiona beamed and reapplied her own lip gloss. "We leave in a week. I'm already packed."

"Can you smuggle me in your luggage?" Madison joked.

Fiona offered Madison some gloss. It was called Shimmer, but Madison didn't want any. She'd only chew it off, like she always chewed off lipstick and nail polish.

The second warning bell rang. They had to hurry.

As they exited the bathroom, the three girls almost smacked right into Hart and Dan, who were rushing off to class, too.

"Whoa," Hart said, avoiding the collision. "Hey, Finnster . . ."

Madison's cheeks turned red and hot. But they didn't talk. No one wanted to be late for class.

Concentrating seemed pointless after that. All

Madison could think of was the way Hart's brown hair looked when they had bumped into each other, the way it was swept over to the side, the way it curled near his neck. No matter how hard she tried to think about math equations, it was Hart and his hairdo that kept popping into her head.

Since Mom was busy working on film edits this week, she'd asked Fiona's dad to give Madison a ride to and from the animal clinic. Mr. Waters agreed. It was on the way to Chet's karate class, which made it convenient for everyone.

While sitting in the Waterses' car, Madison stayed silent in the backseat while Chet and his dad talked sports. Chet looked like a miniature version of his father.

"I can't remember if you told me this or not. Are you playing on any teams, Maddie?" Mr. Waters asked. She *had* told him before, but she didn't mind repeating it.

"No teams," Madison confessed. "I work on the school Web site and now I have the volunteering."

"Well, that's certainly a lot to do," Mr. Waters said. He gave Chet a sidelong glance. "Why don't you stop playing video games and try volunteering?"

"Dad," Chet mumbled.

The Far Hills Animal Shelter and Clinic appeared at the top of a steep road, and Mr. Waters pulled up in front.

"Thanks, Mr. Waters!" Madison said as she jumped out. "Bye, Chet!"

Inside the waiting room, chaos reigned. Big dogs sniffed little dogs while shivering cats extended claws and hissed from inside their kitty carryalls. One boy held on to a box so tightly his knuckles had turned white.

Doctor Wing read a name from his chart, and the white-knuckled boy jumped up.

"The python won't eat," the boy said loudly. Madison shuddered to think of the clammy snake curled up inside the box. She'd seen big snakes last summer on her trip to Brazil with Mom, and they gave her the jeebies.

Peeling the box gently from the boy's grasp, Dr. Wing disappeared into an examining room.

"Hello?" Madison chirped over the front counter. An elderly woman was helping Eileen behind the counter. As she turned around, Madison could read Eileen's T-shirt today: LEMUR ALONE! SAVE THE RAIN FOREST! Madison wondered how many shelves Eileen probably needed to keep her shirt collection in order. On Tuesday, she had admitted to having ninety-four T-shirts.

Madison followed Eileen into a paneled office just off the waiting room. Dan was sitting there behind a computer terminal. Madison plopped down into the one empty chair next to him.

"Hey," he said without turning from the monitor.

"Dan's going to show you how to keep updates on the animals in the shelter and clinic, Maddie. We log all our information onto this database. Okay, hon? See you in an hour or so," she said, winking and shutting the door behind her.

Dan punched a few more keys to pause the screen. "This is like control central for the clinic. It's way cool."

"I thought volunteers just fed and watered the animals," Madison said.

"Being a volunteer here means all kinds of stuff. I figured you might like doing the computer work, since you're so good at it. Dr. Wing said something to my mother, too. He knows you help with the school Web site," Dan said.

Madison was impressed that they would have considered that. She still wanted to know when she'd be doing some big-time animal rescuing, but she didn't want to ask too many questions.

Dan stuffed half a doughnut into his mouth and wiped the corners with his sleeve. "Okay," he mumbled, still chewing. "You gotta enter the password here. It's *Falcon* this week. Dr. Wing changes it all the time."

"*Falcon*. Got it," Madison said, watching his every move. "You have . . . uh . . . jelly on your face, Dan." She giggled.

Dan blushed and grabbed another napkin.

They proceeded to the main directory of the database, which included descriptions and photos of the animals who had been brought into the shelter for rescue. It also featured a running tally of supplies for the animals and the animal clinic, a roster of volunteers and their schedules, and much more.

"Hey, that's me!" Madison said when she saw her name as she scrolled down a page. It said: *After school, schedule permitting.* Most junior high and high school students had the same notation.

Dan pointed to a list of supplies and explained to Madison how to add and subtract information based on what was being used in the veterinary office. If Madison used up a bin of kibble, she needed to enter that one bag of kibble was used on the computer.

"My mom set it up so we'd keep track. It saves her time," Dan explained. "It's cool being responsible for stuff, ya know?"

"I know what you mean," Madison said, eyes fixed on the screen.

Dan pulled up another page with the special form the clinic would fill out if a dog got sick.

"If you're checking on a dog or cat or whatever and they look sick, just look at this and you know what questions to ask. Like, 'Does the animal have difficulty keeping food down?' You can fill this out here, hit send, and blam! Dr. Wing gets it in his e-mailbox. Coolness, right?"

"Cool," Madison said. "What's that page?" She pointed to another document named Waiting Lists & Foster Care.

"The clinic is pretty small, so Dr. Wing can't take in all the animals. So sometimes people in Far Hills give animals foster homes."

One by one, they went over other basic procedures. Madison suddenly understood why having volunteers was so important. There was a lot going on behind the scenes. For every yelping pup in the kennel room, there was a sick cat on an examination table. For every person who wanted to adopt a stray, there were three strays that couldn't find a home.

She watched Dan closely. Most kids at school thought of Dan as the overweight kid who only wanted brownies and never played sports. In reality, he knew about computers and animals of all kinds. Madison decided right there that Dan Ginsburg was cooler than cool.

"Ya know, I want to be a vet when I grow up," Dan said.

"I would love to be a vet, too," Madison said. "Or maybe a movie producer like my mom."

"You could make movies about animals," Dan said. "Like *Jaws*."

"*Jaws?*" Madison gasped. She knew that was the scary movie about a man-eating shark.

Dan chuckled to himself. "Just kidding."

After working on the database some more, Dan and Madison were on their way to becoming friends. It seemed funny to have so much in common with a boy, but Madison was thankful for it.

"DR. WING!"

There was a sudden shout coming from the waiting room. Dan recognized his mom's voice, and they jumped up to see what was the matter.

Eileen was kneeling on the steps near the door. In her arms she was cradling a small dog, trembling and whining. Her fur was all matted and dirty. Her sad eyes were wet with tears. It looked like she had burns on her coat and tail, too. Madison wanted to look away. The dog was obviously hurting.

"Oh, man," Dan groaned.

"Dan." Eileen shot him a look.

Dr. Wing rushed up. "Another one, huh?" he said to Eileen. She nodded and sighed. The dog whined a little louder as more people gathered.

Dan whispered to Madison, "Sometimes people abandon their dogs right here, right on the clinic steps."

"People just leave the dogs alone here?" Madison asked.

Dr. Wing and Eileen brought the abandoned animal into an examining room to see what damage had been done. The dog needed a bath and medicine right away. It was a mixed breed, called a schnoodle. The name was a perfect fit for the miniature dog's mix of schnauzer and poodle. Dr. Wing checked the dog's temperature, breaths per minute, and heart rate. Everything was racing.

"Gums are swollen," Dr. Wing said, checking

inside the dog's mouth. "Needs hydration."

Dan whispered to Madison, "Most dogs that come in off the street haven't eaten, and they're all dehydrated."

"Irregular breathing," Eileen said aloud, stroking the dog's coat.

"Let's get an IV over here," Dr. Wing said.

Madison gawked. It was like an emergency-room TV show, only with animals.

"You two need to go back to the other room now," Eileen said gently, shutting the door.

Dan shook his head. "I've seen that happen so many times."

"It's so sad," Madison said. "What will you name this one, Dan?"

"Good question. Hmmm . . ." Dan thought for a moment.

"She looks like the color of cinnamon," Madison said. "And sweet, like cinnamon sugar."

"Sugar! I like *that*. Mom will, too," Dan said.

In the back of the clinic, there was an office that was decorated more like a bedroom or a den. That was where Dr. Wing or someone on his staff would sometimes stay overnight if they were worried about an animal. Tonight the doctor was staying there himself to watch the new arrival.

Everyone wanted to make sure Sugar the schnoodle made it safely through the night.

Madison wished she could stay over, too.

Chapter 6

 The **Mayflower**

Whew. I was afraid Egg would forget our
meeting for social studies, but he didn't.
He was just LATE. We finally picked our
project (the **Mayflower**) for Mrs. Belden's
class. Wow! He had so many great ideas
about building this model of the actual
Mayflower ship and putting it onto
PowerPoint. I hate to say that I never
expected him to be good at this kind of
thing, but he is good. Wicked good.

Egg really and truly needs this project
to raise his social studies grade, so the
pressure's on. I already printed a list off
a Web site that explains how the real ship
was built back in its day. Materials I
think we need so far: poster board,

clear-dry glue, board chips for the boat.
     Sometimes I think I'm doing my
extra-credit project with a PARTNER with a
missing PART! LOL. But he did say he was
sorry for being late twice. I guess I'll
get over being annoyed eventually.

When Madison couldn't think about the extra
credit anymore, she opened the file on the disk with
her English essay instead. She could finish typing on
the library and media center computer. This was such
a quiet spot! She had to rush, however, so she could
still go downstairs to meet Fiona after soccer practice.
Mr. Waters was taking Madison to the Far Hills Animal
Shelter and Clinic again this afternoon. This family
was becoming her regular ride for her extra trips to
the clinic. Madison had explained to Mom about the
sick schnoodle and how much she wanted to be with
her. As long as Madison got her work done, Mom said
she could go more than once a week.

"Hop in, Maddie," Mr. Waters said.

"Is Fiona around?" Madison asked, poking her
head inside the front seat. She saw Fiona's soccer
bag inside the minivan.

Mr. Waters shook his head. "Around the corner.
Get in and we'll ride over there," he said, helping
push her backpack between the seat and the floor.
Madison slid the door shut behind her.

"Fiona went to get her brother," Mr. Waters said,
driving around to the other side of school.

There, by the entrance and exit to the boys' gym, Fiona was waving and waiting with Chet. Next to them, sitting on his propped-up backpack, was Egg.

Madison waved. Egg smiled.

"Hey, partner," he joked as he got into the backseat behind Madison.

"Whatever," Madison quipped. "When you're not *late*, anyway . . ."

"Cut me a break, will ya?" Egg said.

"Hey, Maddie!" Fiona said, sliding open the door and jumping inside.

Chet rode up in front next to Mr. Waters.

"You're like a limo service, Dad," Fiona quipped. The truth was that Mr. Waters worked half days at the office and half days at home, so he could afford to get out afternoons for chauffeuring duties.

Madison twisted around to see Egg. "Why are you here, anyway?"

"Secret mission," Egg cracked.

"Yeah, secret mission to eliminate annoying twin sisters . . ." Chet started to say. Fiona slugged him on the shoulder.

"And friends of twin sisters," Egg added.

Madison shot him a look.

"Now, now. Settle down, kids," Mr. Waters said. He changed the subject. "So how was practice, Fiona?"

"Fine."

"What's your coach got planned for a winning season?"

"I don't know," Fiona said because she didn't feel like being interrogated. "Dad, can we get ice cream?"

"Oh yeah, Dad. Can we?" Chet asked.

While Fiona and Chet pleaded for an ice cream detour, Madison gazed out the minivan window . . . far, far away as she could. Outside, Far Hills was in the process of relandscaping parks and repaving its main thoroughfare. One part of the downtown area had a dog run so owners could go give their dogs exercise. As they passed by, she counted five or six dogs chasing Frisbees in clouds of dirt. Before Madison realized it, they'd arrived at the clinic.

"Here we are!" Mr. Waters announced as they pulled up in front. As Madison got out of the car, Fiona and Chet waved, but Egg made a funny face. She wasn't sure why. He really could be so annoying.

"Good-bye!" Madison skipped away.

They drove off.

"Hellooooo?" Madison called out when she walked into the clinic. She didn't hear any people or animals right away. "Eileen? Dan? Dr. Wing?"

Madison walked into the office first. Dan wasn't around. She could hear Dr. Wing and a nurse in one of the examination rooms. Madison checked the animal cages. Most of the dogs were calm and quiet. Mr. Wollensky was back there today, grooming one of the Yorkie terriers who had been staying at the clinic for a while. Madison greeted them both and proceeded to read the charts in front of some of the other cages.

Blinky, arrived October 15, abandoned, eyes healing.

Blinky blinked and panted hello. Madison could tell he was getting much better. So were the dogs in connecting cages.

Pavlov, arrived September 30, neglected. Handle with care.

Pavlov was lying there, chest still heaving with uneasy rhythms. He wasn't hurt on the outside. Pavlov was hurt on the inside. Madison imagined how much he'd suffered before getting to this place. It made her so sad.

Then she came to Sugar the schnoodle's cage.

Since Sugar had been discovered, Dr. Wing and Eileen had taken extra-special care of her. Her coat looked shinier now. Most of the tangles were combed out. Without the scabs and matted fur, Sugar looked more like a spunky dog—rather than just a mess.

Sugar stuck her nose right up to the cage door and sniffed. When Madison put her finger a little closer, Sugar licked it gently.

"Hello, Sugar," Madison said. "Schnoodle-oodleeee-oh." The dog cowered a little, but still came back to investigate Madison's scent.

"WHO are you talking to?" Dan asked, walking into the back area. "You sound like a yodeler."

"Dan!" Madison jumped, a little taken off guard. "I didn't know you were here!"

"So who are you talking to?"

"Just the schnoodle. She's so pretty today," Madison said. "I'm glad I named her Sugar."

"Yeah, she looks way better than before," Dan said, slinging his backpack onto the floor and walking over to the cages. "You were in pretty bad shape before, but now you're one hot dog."

Madison groaned. "That's so lame, Dan."

"It was funny! Come on!" Dan snickered. He stuck his fingertips under Sugar's nose and she licked them.

"What happened to her?" Madison asked. "Do you think she was abused?"

Dan nodded. "My mom says so. We get all kinds of dogs here with problems like burns from cigarettes, broken bones, and not being fed. People can be so mean. I don't get it. How could you be mean to an animal?"

Madison's heart sank. She couldn't believe it, either. As the afternoon went on, Madison found herself drawn to Sugar's cage more than the cages of any other dogs. This schnauzer-poodle loved all the attention.

"I'm a little surprised at how quickly she's recovering, to tell ya the truth," Dan's mother said when she saw Madison and Sugar together. "Usually these dogs need time before they cling on to ya. You must have something special, Maddie."

"She's the one who's special," Madison said.

"Yup, this one seems to have a bond with you," Eileen said. "You're turning into a special volunteer in only a short time. I'm impressed, and so is Dr. Wing."

Madison dropped her head, a little self-conscious from the sudden attention. She scratched the top of Sugar's head.

"Well, I mean it," Eileen said. "Right away you were a natural at this, and we're very lucky to have you be a part of our little Far Hills Animal Clinic family."

"Thanks, Eileen," Madison said softly. She looked at Eileen's T-shirt, which read LOVE A PET, LOVE A VET.

Madison felt loved, too.

When Madison came home, she sprawled on the bed to check her e-mail. She loved the way Sugar had nuzzled, snuggled, and *needed* Madison. Bigwheels would love hearing all about it.

Phin tried to climb onto the bed, but she shooed him away.

"I'm busy right now, Phinnie," Madison cooed.

Phin barked and got down on all fours like he would pounce. This pug wanted to play. But then he gave up and crawled under Madison's desk.

There was only one message. It was from Dad.

```
From: JeffFinn
To: MadFinn
Subject: Let's Talk
Date: Thurs 16 Nov 5:03 PM
```
Honey bear, we need to talk soon. I tried leaving a message, but tell your mother the machine is broken. I know you are at the animal hospital. I hope that is fun. Please call me tonight when you get in.

A joke for you: What do you get when you cross a turkey and an octopus? Ha ha.

I'll tell you the answer when you call!

Love you,

Dad

Madison shut off the computer and dashed downstairs to the living room. She checked the answering machine, which was blinking frantically. She dialed Dad's number.

What did Dad have to tell her that he couldn't say in e-mail?

Dad would never put important things in e-mail. He liked to talk about things in person, or at least on the phone.

"Hey, sweetie," Dad whispered as he picked up the phone. "How's my little girl?" He always called her that, much to Madison's dismay. She thought of herself as slightly more sophisticated, especially since junior high began.

"What's up with you, Dad?" Madison asked back. "By the way, the answer to your riddle is you get a lot of drumsticks when you cross an octopus and a turkey!"

Dad laughed. Then he told her about work being busy as ever. He had purchased a new wok for his kitchen.

"I was thinking about making stir-fry turkey this Thanksgiving," Dad said.

"Very funny, Dad," Madison replied, half laughing.

He followed up with another joke. "Hey, Maddie, why was the turkey included as a member of the band?"

"What band?" Madison groaned. "Okay. Why?"

"Because he had all the drumsticks." Dad laughed out loud. "Get it?"

It was maybe the dumbest joke Dad had told in the longest time, but suddenly Madison felt choked up. She wasn't sure if she got teary with the mention of Thanksgiving, or if she had a sudden surge of missing Dad, since he hadn't been around much lately.

"I really wish we could—" Madison swallowed

the words. "I wish we could spend Thanksgiving together, Dad."

Dad got silent on the other end of the phone line. "Gee, Maddie—"

Madison interrupted. "Oh, forget I said that. That was so dumb."

"No. What's going on? Is something bugging you?" Dad asked.

"You mean besides homework and my friend Egg?" Madison blurted, trying to shift gears and change the subject.

"Huh? You lost me," Dad said.

Madison took a deep breath. "I miss you, Dad. So much."

She could hear him take a deep breath through the phone, too. "I know," Dad said. "I know you do."

"So why can't I spend Thanksgiving with you—and your family?" Madison asked.

"My family? What? Madison, we've been over this. The lawyers' arrangement says—"

"I don't care what it says," Madison cried. "I don't want to spend Thanksgiving in this house if YOU can't be here. Thanksgiving is supposed to be a family holiday, and I don't want to spend Thanksgiving alone with no one but Mom because . . . I just don't want to. I don't."

Dad took another loud breath. "Madison?" he asked sweetly.

Madison was afraid of what he might say. She'd let all her feelings come tumbling out at once. They'd taken her by surprise.

"Why don't we talk about it at dinner tomorrow night," Dad said, trying to change the subject. "And about that dinner . . ."

Madison gulped. "Yeah?"

"I was going to bring Stephanie," Dad said.

Madison was silent.

Dad quickly recovered. "Unless you don't want me to. I mean, it can just be you and me alone, Maddie. You tell me."

But Madison didn't quibble. She agreed to have dinner with them both. It was hard to have anything but good feelings for Dad's girlfriend when she always came with a little present for Madison like flea-market earrings made from glass and asked lots of fun questions about school and boys and life in general. Stephanie seemed so interested in what Madison thought and believed. She was pretty, too, with perfect fingernails.

"Hey!" Mom walked in, carrying an armful of groceries. "Who's on the phone?"

"No one," Madison fibbed, covering the receiver. Then she admitted the truth. "Just Dad."

"Oh," Mom said, walking into the kitchen. Madison could hear her pushing vegetables into the refrigerator bins.

"Bye, Dad," Madison said into the phone quickly.

"I have to go help Mom make dinner. She just got home."

Mom asked her to help boil water for the ziti while she cut up lettuce and tomatoes for salad.

"I was talking to Dad about Thanksgiving," Madison said, filling a pot.

"Oh," Mom replied. "Does he have plans?"

Madison put water on the stove and added a little olive oil to separate the boiling pasta. It was a trick Gramma had shown her. "Actually, he didn't really talk about Thanksgiving."

Madison wasn't sure why she lied, but she did.

"Oh," Mom said for a third time. "Well, I'm sure he'll be spending it with that girlfriend of his."

"Her name is Stephanie," Madison added. She could tell when Mom didn't want to talk. Whenever she "forgot" someone's name, it meant the subject should be changed.

"So where's Phin?" Mom asked. "We should walk him before supper."

"Phin?" Madison whirled around, half expecting to find him by her feet, but the pug wasn't there. "I dunno. I saw him a while ago. . . ."

"He's been acting funny lately. Have you noticed?" Mom said. She had been taking Phin for long walks during the afternoons when Madison went to volunteer at the shelter.

"I haven't noticed anything," Madison said.

"It's probably nothing." Mom shook her head.

"He's probably just a little jealous. You're giving all your attention to the other dogs now."

Madison giggled. "Mom, don't be ridiculous. Phinnie doesn't know what I'm doing."

The phone rang again and Madison grabbed it. "House of Finn," she cried into the receiver spontaneously. She looked across at Mom, who was chuckling a little now, too. Lately they'd been goofing around when answering the phone. One night Mom had picked it up and said, "Finn Land." They almost fell on the floor, laughing so hard.

But Egg was the one on the phone, and he didn't get what was funny at all.

"House of what?" Egg said.

"Oh, it's you." Madison faked a growl.

"What is your problem, Maddie?" he asked. "You can't still be mad about me being late. I said sorry like a hundred times already."

"You said sorry twice. That is not a hundred times," Madison said.

She and Egg bickered some more. Ten minutes later, they came to an agreement to meet the next day after school to talk about the *Mayflower*. They'd meet in Mrs. Wing's computer lab so they could use the Internet. No one would bother them.

"Don't forget, Egg, please be on time. I don't want to wait around forever," Madison said.

"Yeah, yeah, I KNOW," he grumbled.

Madison tried to soften the tone a little bit. "This

project will be awesome—I know it," she said reassuringly.

"Of course it will!" Egg said. He sounded encouraged, so she hung up the phone and sat down to dinner.

"Is this a little sticky, or is it me?" Mom asked when she tasted dinner. "We'll keep practicing, right, honey bear?"

The pasta was overcooked, but Madison ate two helpings.

Right before bed, Madison powered up her laptop.

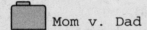 Mom v. Dad

Rude Awakening: It's hard to be fair and square when you feel like part of a triangle.

Am I being fair to Mom? She is trying so hard to make dinners and to be nice letting me volunteer and taking Phin for walks. Do I say thank you and please enough? I made this whole huge deal about wanting to spend Thanksgiving with Dad and now . . . everything is different. I just want to have turkey on Thanksgiving and to make them both happy. Am I making Mom sad? Is Dad sad? How am I supposed to be?

Madison hit SAVE and logged on to bigfishbowl.com. She was in search of a friend—and a little perspective. Bigwheels was online! She Insta-Messaged her keypal, hoping for some wiser-than-wise advice.

```
<Bigwheels>: hi there
<MadFinn>: what r u doing up???
   Ur online!
<Bigwheels>: Im bored w/homewk
<MadFinn>: HELP
<Bigwheels>: my teachers gave a
   really hard assignment
<MadFinn>: u work all the time
<Bigwheels>: IYSS
<MadFinn>: I don't mean in a bad
   way
<Bigwheels>: :>)
<MadFinn>: E2EG I wrote to ask
   advice about my parents
<Bigwheels>: what is wrong are they
   fighting
<MadFinn>: What will I do at
   Thanksgiving with Mom it's a big
   mess
<Bigwheels>: so don't have dinner
   w/Mom
<MadFinn>: but I will hurt her
   feelings if I don't
<Bigwheels>: no u won't, he is ur
   Dad she will understand that is
   her job right?
<MadFinn>: yeah but she'll be alone
```

```
<Bigwheels>: so don't WORRY
<MadFinn>: thanx for ur help
<Bigwheels>: what r u doing 4 ur
   project in school u never told me
<MadFinn>: top secret :-#
<Bigwheels>: LOL I have a project
   too BTW
<MadFinn>: really??
<Bigwheels>: I am writing a paper
   on Wampanoag Indians
<MadFinn>: have you ever been to an
   Indian reservation
<Bigwheels>: no but I have read a
   lot of bks
<MadFinn>: ZZZZZZZZZZZZZ
<Bigwheels>: r u bored?
<MadFinn>: no just sleepy THANKS
   sooo much 4 ur help
<Bigwheels>: sweet dreams
```

Madison logged off her computer and got under the covers. She pictured herself walking Phin and Sugar and Pavlov and Blinky and the rest of the dogs at the same time. She was pulling their leashes and laughing in the November breeze.

This wasn't just any dream.

It was a sweeter-than-sweet dream.

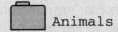 Animals

Rude Awakening: The not-so-dreamy thing about dreams is that you wake up.

I would rather spend more time with animals than anyone else these days.

Today I had a yucky quiz in math that I was 100 percent unprepared for! Grrrr. I should have studied harder and I wish I'd studied harder BUT I haven't had time. I have been going to the clinic more than once a week. I have to make time to study more. I don't want Mom to tell me that I have to stop going to the clinic!

Animals understand me way better than Mom and Dad do. Better than anyone.

Madison checked the clock in Mrs. Wing's classroom and then saved the update to her Animals file. It was a Friday afternoon, and Madison and Egg had made specific arrangements to discuss their extra-credit social studies project. Here. Now.

Where was he?

Madison glanced through the pile of books she'd borrowed from the library. They were stacked on the desk in front of her. One book was a retelling of the entire *Mayflower* journey with reenactment photos. Another book included a complete list of passengers. A Thanksgiving craft workbook even had instructions on making a diorama of the actual *Mayflower* ship.

Madison hoped Egg would come with inspired Thanksgiving ideas of his own that could complement hers. That's what being partners was all about.

Where was he?

By three-thirty, Egg still hadn't arrived—and Madison got a sinking feeling . . . like *she* was sunk. She bent down to grab her orange bag. As she sat up, she saw Egg walking into the computer lab, humming. *Humming?* He didn't seem the least bit concerned.

Madison glared.

"Hey," he said. Then he noticed the look on her face. "What's your problem?" he asked.

Madison stuffed the books into her bag.

"What is it?" Egg asked, taking a seat right next to her. "Is this because I'm late? What time is it? Three o'clock?"

Madison laughed a loud "HA!" and zipped her bag. "Yes, Egg, you are late," she said simply. "Later than late. It's three-thirty-five."

He grabbed her arm. "I lost track of time. Really."

"Well, I'm asking Mrs. Belden for a new partner," Madison said a little dramatically. "I'm asking tomorrow before class."

"Maddie, don't be like that." Egg hung his head. "I said I was sorry and you're dropping me?"

"How can you just forget that we're supposed to meet?"

"I'm so sorry, Maddie. I didn't forget completely."

Madison slung her book bag over her shoulder. "Well, I don't know. That's what you always say."

"Please. We'll do the project. I swear I won't ever be late again," Egg pleaded. "PLEASE?"

Madison put her bag back on the desk. "You mean it?" she said.

Egg nodded. "Cross my heart and stick a needle in my—"

"Yeah, yeah," she said. "But this really is the last time, Egg."

They took seats at the study table in the corner of Mrs. Wing's classroom and opened their notebooks. Madison yanked a small pile of *Mayflower* books and her notebook out of her orange bag.

Egg just sat there, rolling a pencil between his fingers.

He hadn't brought *any* backup materials.

"Wait a minute. You said you were bringing books." Madison tried to remain as calm as possible, but it was getting harder to do that.

"I never said that," Egg replied quickly, a little defensive.

"Yes, you did!" Madison said. "Egg, are you for real?"

Egg rolled his eyes. "I NEVER said that I was bringing any books. *Really.*"

"Thanks for nothing," Madison said under her breath. She stood up, put the books into her bag, and got ready to go for real this time.

Egg followed her out of the classroom into the hallway, but when she continued to ignore him, he turned on his heel and left.

A moment later, Fiona appeared at the lockers. She'd stayed late for indoor soccer practice.

"Weren't you meeting Egg after school?" Fiona asked. She always wanted the inside information on Egg's every move.

Right now the last person Madison wanted to talk about was Egg.

"I absolutely refuse to even say his name," Madison snapped, walking fast. Fiona hustled alongside her.

"What's wrong?" Fiona said. "Are you mad

about something? Are you mad at me?"

Madison stopped. She apologized by giving Fiona a quick hug. She hadn't meant to snap. Everything this Thanksgiving season was leaving Madison extra stressed.

"I'm sorry," Madison said. "I'm just feeling a little stressed out. How was soccer?"

"I got two goals in our scrimmage. I like indoor almost as much as outdoor soccer."

"You wanna walk home together?" Madison asked. She was ready to leave school—and the Egg incident—far behind her. It felt better walking home with a BFF like Fiona.

"Maddie, what's up with you and Dan?" Fiona asked. "I meant to ask you in school today. I see you guys together a lot lately."

Madison laughed. "Me and Dan? What do you mean?"

"Aimee and I were wondering if maybe you like him," Fiona said. "You've been hanging out with him at the clinic all week. And he's always talking about you, too."

"What? I don't like Dan *that* way," Madison said. "He's like a brother."

"He's not like MY brother." Fiona smiled. "But that's a good thing. . . ."

"How's your project coming along with Daisy for social studies?" Madison asked.

Fiona started babbling about how she and Daisy

were planning an amazing oral report on Sarah Hale. Sarah Hale was a woman who spoke up about the values of Thanksgiving during the Civil War. She helped convince President Abraham Lincoln to declare it a national holiday.

"I think I might dress up like Sarah Hale and Daisy might dress up like Abe Lincoln. We're not sure yet. It's been so much fun."

"You're kidding, right?" Madison moaned.

"And we're going to read part of Lincoln's Thanksgiving Proclamation from the war, too. I almost forgot that part," Fiona added.

Madison waved good-bye when they got to Fiona's house. Walking away, she buttoned up her coat a little because the air was crisp. It was hard to believe that November was more than halfway over.

Much to her surprise, Dad was waiting in the driveway, arms folded, when Madison wandered up.

"I know we said five," he said. "But I decided to come by early."

Madison looked at her watch. "An *hour* early?" she exclaimed.

"Why don't *you* run inside and get yourself together," he said softly. "I'll wait out here."

"Why don't you just come inside and wait, Daddy? Mom won't mind. She's so busy working, anyway."

Cautiously Dad approached the front door, trying to catch a glimpse of whatever might await him inside. He hardly ever came back into 5 Blueberry Street anymore. The Big D was like a big roadblock.

Mom opened the door wide. "Hello, there," she said. Phin squiggled out and went right for Dad, who leaned down to scratch the top of his coarse fur head.

"Hello, Frannie," Dad said in a soft voice.

Mom opened the door wider and tried to smile. She ushered him inside.

Even though Mom and Dad were acting perfectly nice to each other, Madison felt all awkward when they were in a room together. She never knew what to say.

"I have to change," Madison blurted.

Dad smiled. "Good idea."

"Yes, we like our child dressed when she leaves the house," Mom said.

Madison shrugged and dashed upstairs. She could hear Mom and Dad still chuckling moments afterward. It was strange to have them together in the house.

Quickly she ransacked her closet and pulled out her jean skirt with the purple patches and slipped into a pale yellow sweater and dark grape-colored clogs. She piled her hair into a purple clip and put on her moonstone earrings and moonstone ring, too. It was her special, lucky jewelry she'd gotten from Dad *and* Mom on separate occasions.

Phinnie was in the bedroom with Madison when

she got ready, but he didn't scurry over to her for kisses like he normally did. He lay on the floor, paws stretched out in front, eyes glazed over. He looked sad, Madison thought. She patted him on the head.

"Phinnie, what's the matter?" she asked.

He rolled over onto his back and sat up, nuzzling her free hand.

"I have to go, Phinnie," Madison said, standing herself. "I'm sorry. I have to go to dinner with Dad."

Phin lay back down in the exact same spot. Madison headed slowly back downstairs.

Mom and Dad were standing in the hallway, in almost the exact same positions they'd been in when Madison charged up the stairs. They were talking about the weather.

Madison reappeared, taking two steps at a time. "I'm ready to go!" She waved to Mom with a big grin. "See you later."

"Have a nice time, honey bear," Mom said, kissing Madison's cheek. "Good-bye, Jeffrey."

Dad said good-bye and then put his arm around Madison as they walked back to the car.

"You look very pretty this evening, Maddie," he said. As usual, he noticed when she was trying to wear something special. "Especially the earrings," he added, winking.

"Dad . . . why do you and Mom always argue?" Madison asked as they drove away.

Dad seemed confused. "Argue? What are you

talking about? We were talking about the Weather Channel."

"Well, it's just so weird when you guys are together now," Madison said.

"What are you talking about, Maddie? You know real arguing. That's what your mother and I used to do every day when we were—"

"I know," Madison cut him off. "But the thing is, Dad, it all feels the same to me. It's just too weird the way you talk—about the dumbest things in the world."

"We're just being polite, Maddie," Dad said. "Neither of us wants any more conflicts, believe me. You have to stop worrying. It has nothing to do with you."

Madison really wanted to believe him, but she just wasn't sure.

When they arrived at the restaurant, Stephanie met them in the lounge by a big grand piano. A man with a salt-and-pepper beard was growling some song about love.

"You look gorgeous!" Stephanie said, leaning down to give Madison a squeeze. "Love that purple skirt!"

Madison blushed a little and mumbled, "Thank you."

"Let's get our table, shall we, ladies?" Dad said, grinning. He had pep in his step as he led them over to the maitre d's station.

"This is an elegant restaurant, Jeff," Stephanie cooed during appetizers. She kept kissing his cheek, but Madison didn't mind as much as usual.

"Did you cut your hair?" Madison asked Stephanie. It was newly set into a bob of brown curls that rested just on her shoulders.

Stephanie threw back her head and all the curls bounced like on some shampoo commercial. "Do you like it?"

"You look gorgeous!" Madison teased. "You do. Really and truly."

As dinner passed, Madison felt very comfortable with Dad and Stephanie, more than she ever had before. She began to wonder about Thanksgiving. Maybe she should be spending it with *them*?

Madison wanted to find the right moment to bring up the subject, but then Dad started talking about Thanksgiving on his own. It was almost as if Madison had willed him to bring up the subject.

"Stephanie was asking me about our holiday plans, Madison," he said. "Now, I know that you are supposed to spend Thanksgiving with your mother."

"Yeah?" Madison said.

"Your dad and I wondered if maybe you'd spend it with us instead?" Stephanie asked.

She didn't know how to respond. Even though she'd been thinking about that very thing, she was taken by surprise. She awkwardly picked at a leaf of lettuce on her plate.

"I know we have to ask your mom and all that," Dad said. "And we're not asking you to choose or anything. I just got to thinking when we talked the other day. . . ."

"Would your mom mind?" Stephanie asked, trying to catch Madison's eye.

"What do you think, Maddie?" Dad asked.

Madison took a long pause before answering. "Well . . ." she started to say.

"No pressure," Dad said.

Stephanie spoke up. "He's right, Maddie. It's just a suggestion."

Madison took time to think about it. Dozens of thoughts whizzed through her mind, thoughts about Gramma Helen's busted hip and stuffing and cranberry sauce and what her best friends would be doing on Thanksgiving day—like Fiona's going to California and Aimee's hanging around the house, watching football.

How should she respond to Dad and Stephanie's question? She didn't know what to do. Say yes? The words wouldn't come.

Madison felt like such a turkey.

known have to say your chop and stuff.
Dad said, "And we're not asking you to choose or
anything. We got to the only reason we talked (or
whatever."

Chapter 8

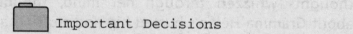

Important Decisions

Rude Awakening: To go or not to go? That
is the question.

Tonight at dinner everything changed
inside my head. I want to go with Dad and
Stephanie, but I don't want to leave Mom
all alone for Thanksgiving. What am I
supposed to do?

Mom was waiting for me in the living
room when I walked in tonight and I said
something dorky about how I ate pork chops
for dinner. That was all I could say.

And there she was sitting on the sofa,
pulling out all our old Thanksgiving
decorations, like this funny-looking
cornucopia I made in kindergarten, and all
I can think about was how sad I feel this

year. How can I help decorate if I don't
want to be here?

I really and truly want to be with Dad.
That's my decision. Better get to sleep.

The next morning at breakfast, Mom was *still*
pulling out Thanksgiving decorations. Inside an old,
ratty shopping bag she'd rediscovered orange and
brown grosgrain ribbons and cardboard turkeys with
tears along the edges and faded spots where they'd
been used over the years.

"I pulled this down from the attic," Mom said,
smiling. "Turkeys, pumpkins, you know the stuff we
always put up when you were a kid."

Madison took a big swallow of cereal. "Mn-
hhuhh," she said, chewing and nodding at the same
time. "Mn-hhuhh, I know."

"Can you believe we still have this?" Mom said,
pulling a plastic Pilgrim out of the bag. One foot was
almost eaten off.

Phin got up on his hind legs when he saw the
chewed-up Pilgrim and started to growl. Madison
nearly spit out her mouthful of cereal.

"He's still mad at it?" she asked.

The plastic Pilgrim had been a decoration that
was part of a Plymouth Rock set Dad bought when
Phin was just a puppy. He had been afraid of the set
at first, but then he'd munched on each plastic figure one by one. The Pilgrim Mom was holding was
the only one rescued from the bunch.

"Grrrrrrrrrrrrrrrrrooooof!" Phinnie yapped again. "Rowrrorororoo!"

Mom and Madison started to laugh. It felt so good to laugh.

"Phinnie," Madison said, grabbing for his collar. But he didn't pay attention. He scooted over and jumped onto Mom's lap instead.

"Hey, there, wiggler," Mom teased, scratching his head.

Madison slurped down the rest of her cereal. Putting up decorations was not what she wanted to do, but the idea of telling Mom the truth about Dad's invitation was something she wanted to do even *less*. What was there to celebrate? She thought of the devastated look on Mom's face when the Thanksgiving truth was revealed: Madison wanted to spend Thanksgiving with Dad. This decision was final . . . right?

Mom's work phone rang, and she went into the office. Phin followed her inside with his nose in the air. Normally he would have stayed close to Madison and begged for a cookie.

"Phinnie?" Madison watched the dog follow Mom. She sighed and went upstairs to open a brand-new file on her laptop.

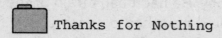 Thanks for Nothing

Rude Awakening: I've decided to quit Thanksgiving cold turkey.

First of all, I'm mad at Egg. And Mom
and Dad are about to get really mad at each
other because of me. Even Phin is moping
around! What do I have to be thankful for?

Thanksgiving should be way easier than
it is. Why do I feel a whole lot of thanks
for NOTHING? YUCK.

**As Madison hit SAVE, a brand new e-message
marked *priority* popped up on the screen. It had a
red exclamation point next to it, which meant "read
me now."**

From: Bigwheels
To: MadFinn
Subject: NOW IT'S UR TURN!
Date: Sat 18 Nov 9:25 AM

How is the animal shelter? What
kinds of dogs are there? Other
animals, too?

I have a funny story to tell. I
ALMOST CAME TO NEW YORK for
Thanksgiving! Instead of our big
family thing we almost decided to go
visit my other grandma on the East
Coast. What if we came there? I
wonder if you and I would ever be
able to meet F2F. My mom says
someday we will. She knows all about
you BTW. Does ur mom know about me?

It's so funny b/c usually you write
and say I miss you b/c I am the
lame one who hasn't e-mailed. But
now it's me who misses you like
you're a new part of my family or
something.

Where r u?

Yours till the autumn leaves,

Bigwheels

P.S. Whatever happened to your
crush? Write back soon. I'm waiting.

Since the note had just been sent, Madison typed
back an Insta-Message quickly, hoping to catch her
buddy online. "Bigwheels, where are you?" she
asked aloud, typing as fast as her fingers would go.
She scanned the alphabetical list of names in the
bigfishbowl.com waiting room.

Amazing23
andrew_mac
AngelFace
Bethiscool
BryanSarah
Email_BOY
f2f2f2f2f
Jessica_01
LittleKevin
MARKIEhockey

Nowhere!

Madison's keypal had vanished as quickly as she'd arrived. Madison reread Bigwheels's e-mail and thought about everything she'd said. Then she went back to the Thanks for Nothing file and reread everything *she'd* said.

There had to be a better way to see things.

Madison just didn't know where to look.

She clicked back to Bigwheels's original e-mail and punched REPLY.

From: MadFinn
To: Bigwheels
Subject: Re: NOW IT'S UR TURN!
Date: Sat 18 Nov 10:06 AM

I can't believe you aren't coming to NY. I wonder if we ever really will meet. That is so weird. I wish sometimes that you lived next door.

The social studies project is better, I guess. My partner isn't taking it as seriously as me, but I think we'll be ok. I wish my family felt more ok, though. What is your family really like? And I mean all the time and not just on Thanksgiving. You know how sometimes people act so different during the holidays? At least my family does. What do you talk about with your family?

BTW my volunteering @ the clinic is awesome. I am soooo close already to this one dog I named Sugar. She is a mixed breed and very friendly. It tickles when she gives me kisses on the hand.

Please write again soon.

Yours till the pork chops (because I had those for dinner last night),

MadFinn

p.s. I still think my crush likes this other girl who happens to be my enemy @ school. I told you that, right? I don't know for sure. Bye!

Late on Saturday afternoon, after walking Phin around the block and working for an hour on a school essay, Madison headed over to the animal shelter and clinic with Mom.

The sky was beginning to cloud up like rain was on the way. Madison brought her raincoat and umbrella just in case. She was always prepared for bad weather, even drizzle. Madison liked to be prepared for as many things as possible.

"I'll pick you up later on," Mom said before driving off. "In a couple of hours, okay?"

"Thanks, Mom," Madison said. "See you later."

Eileen was sitting at the front desk of the clinic with a juice bottle and an empty stare. She seemed tired today, but her shirt read I'M FELINE GREAT! It had an image of a giant, fluffy gray cat and a logo for the National Pet Adoption Service.

Madison walked up to the counter and grabbed the visitor and volunteer sign-in sheet. Dan's name was signed for the morning, which meant he was around somewhere. He was probably in the back, taking care of Sugar the schnoodle or some other pup. She went back to search for him

"Madison," Eileen called after her. "I have to check in with Dr. Wing. Would you please go in back and help Mr. Wollensky with the cages?"

Madison started to walk away.

"Don't forget, it's the weekend," Eileen called after her. "So we don't have many appointments. It should be quiet around here. We just need to feed everyone. I'll be back in a jiffy."

As Eileen hustled out a side door, Madison looked for Mr. Wollensky and Sugar.

She glanced at the cages of animals lined against the wall. The dogs stared back. All of a sudden one howled. Then *all* the dogs started howling in unison.

"Hey!" Madison called out to them. "Shhh! Stop that!"

Then they howled a little louder—even Sugar.

Mr. Wollensky started to laugh. "They have something important to say, yes?"

"I wish they would stop."

Madison begged the animals, "Shhh! Please? Pretty please?" As if they understood a single word she was saying!

"HOWWWWWWWWOOOOOOOOOO," Sugar wailed at the fluorescent light on the ceiling. She wouldn't stop baying.

Mr. Wollensky decided a feeding was probably in order. Maybe one cup each of Happy-Gro Kibble would quiet them? Madison tried to help him by grabbing an oversized container of food from the shelf. She started to measure the kibble out very, very slowly until—

CRASH!

The giant bag of dog food split open and Kibble went streaming all over the floor. Madison stared as kibble rolled under counters and into corners of the room. She threw her hands up with despair.

Mr. Wollensky laughed again. "Oh, my! What mess!"

The dogs kept right on howling.

"Is everything okay in here?" A nurse from the front desk came back to the kennel area. She looked worried.

Mr. Wollensky had everything under control in moments. The dogs stopped howling, too, and started eating. "Everything good," he said, waving the nurse back to the front. "We under control."

Madison collapsed onto a nearby chair and put

her head in her hands. "That was a close call," she told herself. Suddenly she felt a wet nose on her hand.

"You have a friend who wants to play," Mr. Wollensky said, handing Sugar's leash to Madison.

Sugar *was* a new friend, Madison thought. Sugar prodded Madison with her paw like she wanted to be picked up.

"What are you doing?" Madison asked, petting the dog's wiry-haired head. Madison stood up and stepped back to play. Unfortunately, she slipped right down, losing her balance on loose kibble that was still on the floor.

PLUNK!

Madison sat there on the floor in a kibble dust daze, a squiggling, wiggling schnoodle jumping on top.

Mr. Wollensky laughed at the sight of her.

"Hey, Mad-i-son!" Dan yelled, coming back into the kennel room. "What are you doing on the floor?"

"Madison! Is everything okay?" Eileen asked, walking in behind him. "Mr. Wollensky, what happened here?"

"She's crying," Dan said to his mom.

But of course Madison wasn't *crying*. Madison was laughing—hard. Sugar's dog kisses *really* tickled.

"We are fine now," Mr. Wollensky said to Eileen. "Madison and I are cleaning up."

Madison smiled at Mr. Wollensky.

"Your mom just called," Eileen said. "She won't be back in time to pick you up, so I'll be giving you a ride home."

But Eileen would do better than just drive Madison home. She offered to stop off at Freeze Palace for ice cream on the way.

While Eileen dashed to the supermarket, Madison and Dan waited outside Freeze Palace. They ate their ice cream on the curb.

"It's cold out today," Madison said.

"There is *never* a bad time for ice cream!" Dan laughed.

Madison walked on the curb like it was a balance beam. Dan tried, too, but he lost his balance. His ice cream scoop plopped into the gutter.

"Aw, no!" Dan cried, looking at his empty cone. "Good-bye, chocolate chips."

A man was walking a giant sheepdog in front of the store.

"Nice dog," Dan said to the owner as he bent down to pet it. When Madison petted the dog, he slobbered all over her arm.

"Look out!" Dan cried. He pointed to her opposite hand, but it was too late. All the dog petting had Madison off balance, too. And now her ice cream had dropped off, too.

"Whoopsie," she said, giggling.

Dan shook his head. "Way to go."

The sheepdog was happy about the accident, however. He was licking the ice cream off the ground.

Madison and Dan laughed. Madison was glad she and Dan were friends.

Chapter 9

Sunday morning Madison got up earlier than usual for a weekend. She had the social studies project on the brain. Today she and Egg had to finish their extra-credit project. *Finally.*

Madison had been collecting a file and notebook of project ideas for almost a week. She'd found a list on the Web that showed the names of all 104 *Mayflower* passengers from 1620. She had read up about storms at sea and sickness on the plantation. There was a separate list of crew members and ship passengers, some of whom had survived and others who had perished.

After eating breakfast, Mom drove Madison over to the Diaz house. It had been Madison's idea to meet there. That way Egg wouldn't be late and he'd *definitely* show up.

When Madison rang the doorbell, it took a moment for anyone to answer. She later found Egg's grandmother, Abuela; his aunt, Tía Ana; his older sister, Mariah; and his mom sitting in the kitchen, reading the paper and talking.

Egg's house was different than Madison's in so many ways. It was smaller in size, but his place was packed with people.

"Hola! Cómo estás?" Señora Diaz chirped when Madison arrived. She poured a tall glass of juice. "Walter *está arriba.*"

Señora Diaz taught Spanish at Far Hills Junior High and always tried to get Madison to practice her Spanish.

"Por favor, siéntate!" Abuela said to Madison, asking her to sit. Abuela had known Madison ever since she had been a little girl. Madison always loved to hear her tell stories.

"Buenos días, Abuela," Madison said, taking a seat. She searched her mind for the right Spanish words.

"Qué linda eres!" Abuela cried. Madison had no idea what she had said. Just then Egg came into the kitchen.

"What did she say?" Madison giggled.

"Abuela says you're pretty," Egg said.

Madison smiled. "Oh." She could tell that just saying those words made Egg a little bit embarrassed.

"*Cómo está escuela?*" Abuela asked Madison. She wanted to hear about school.

"Come on, Abuela, Madison and I have to go," Egg said, wanting to leave the kitchen.

Madison ate a small cookie from a basket on the table and racked her brain for a way to say that it was good. The only phrase she could remember was, "*Dónde está la policía?*" from last week's Spanish class. But no one wanted to find the police, so she said nothing. She and Egg went to his room to practice the extra-credit presentation.

In a terrarium near a large window, Gato puffed out his pink lizard throat as if to say hello. Egg's pet gecko, Gato, was named for the word *cat* in Spanish. Madison always thought it was funny that Egg would name one animal after another. She liked the fact that he had an unusual pet, though.

"So let me show you what I've got up on the computer," Egg said, punching a few keys. "I've been working on this all weekend."

"Whoa." Madison's jaw dropped as the screen came into focus.

Egg had taken the flat model of the *Mayflower* and turned it into a three-dimensional object on-screen. Madison was thrilled. He downloaded the images so they could put them into a special presentation for class.

"Wow, you can see all the rooms inside," she said, admiring it. "Do you think this should be our whole presentation? I thought we could hand out fact sheets, too. It's always good to pass around something."

"Oh," Egg said. "You think so?"

Madison let him scan through a few more pages.

"See?" Egg pointed to the page. "It has three main masts and a poop deck that's very high up. The middle part of the ship is curved really low into the water."

Madison glanced at the computer screen and cross-referenced it with other reading materials on the *Mayflower* she brought along.

"It says here that the ship was called a 'wet ship' because it was mostly in the water. I didn't know that, did you?" Madison asked.

"Huh?" Egg was too busy moving objects around on-screen to be paying any kind of real attention to what Madison was saying.

"Did you know that the place where passengers slept was called the 'tween decks?" Madison asked. "Cool, huh?"

For twenty minutes, Egg and Madison pored through books and searched on the Internet for more ideas on what to write about.

"Maybe we can make a real ship to show in class," Madison said.

"That would be so lame," Egg whined. He thought only something on the computer would knock everyone's socks off.

"What if we brought materials and everyone could watch the computer and then make their own *Mayflower*?" Madison suggested. "Then we'd have both."

"You want this to be an arts-and-crafts project?" he asked. "Maddie, we need to be high-tech. Paste is for first graders."

"No, no," Madison said. She shook her head no. "What about the Pilgrims? They weren't high-tech." Madison wanted to say that sometimes she *liked* making collages and crafts and what was wrong with that?

"Fine, we can make a poster, too," Egg finally agreed.

But they were interrupted all of a sudden.

"WALTER!" Egg's mother's voice bellowed from the other room. "You have another guest!"

Egg ran down the stairs.

Madison heard Egg greet Drew. She could hear Drew explain that he'd just been working on his social studies project over at Ivy Daly's house. She cringed at the thought.

Drew came into Egg's bedroom and flopped onto a chair. "Hey, Maddie, what's up?"

"Um . . . Egg?" Madison asked. "What about our meeting? We just started. Why is Drew here?"

"Well, I guess we'll have to finish up later," Egg said.

"Huh? Later?" Madison felt a little knot of anger work its way up her throat. "What do you mean, 'later'?" she asked. "Can't *Drew* come back *later*?"

"Can't we just finish tomorrow?" Egg asked.

Drew didn't say much of anything.

"What about today, Egg? We've been planning this for almost a week," Madison said. "You promised."

Drew interrupted. "Hey, I can come over another time. You guys are working on the extra-credit thing."

"Nah, we were mostly done," Egg said.

The rising anger knot was now lodged in Madison's throat. She could feel her whole body flush, like when she got embarrassed—only worse.

"Egg, you promised," she repeated.

She wanted to run.

"I promised not to forget any more meetings. This isn't forgetting. It isn't the same thing."

"Fine, then I guess I'll go," Madison said abruptly. She quickly gathered her books and stuffed loose papers into her orange messenger's bag.

"Why don't you stay and play Wrestle Showdown on the computer? You wanna?" Egg asked. "We can do team play since there's three of us."

"No," she said firmly. "E-mail me later. We don't have a lot of time to work on it anymore."

"I know, I know," Egg said, already a little distracted. He was loading the wrestling computer game and setting up the joysticks.

"Hey, Maddie," Drew asked her on the way out. "What's the deal with you and Dan?"

"Huh?" Madison stopped short. She made a face. "What are you talking about?"

"Ivy was just saying some stuff when I was at her house. . ." Drew said.

"Saying *what*?" Madison wrinkled her nose.

"Nothing. Forget I said it," Drew said.

Madison had no idea what Drew was talking about. She scurried out, passing by the kitchen where Abuela, Señora Diaz, and Tía Ana sipped coffees.

"Madison, you just got here! Where is Walter?" Señora Diaz called out.

"Egg is with Drew. We're going to finish later," Madison explained. She smiled at Egg's family. "See you later. I mean, *adiós*."

"*Adiós!*" Egg's grandmother cried.

Madison lifted the bag of *Mayflower* books over her shoulder and walked toward home. It weighed more than usual, so she took slower steps. There was no big rush to get anywhere right now.

As her house came into view, Madison squinted. Dad's car was in the driveway, which seemed strange, since she wasn't meeting him for dinner or any special occasion.

Madison crept toward the front porch entrance. She'd sneak up the stoop and take them by surprise. What were they saying? The living-room window was cracked open, so Madison could hear voices clearly on the porch without being seen by anyone. She crouched down and listened to Mom and Dad talking. This time, they weren't just chatting about the weather.

Mom and Dad were discussing Thanksgiving. Mom was telling Dad how she wanted to let Madison go with him and Stephanie, since that seemed to be what Madison wanted. Madison listened real close.

She could not believe her ears.

Madison couldn't remember a recent time when they'd ever been this nice while talking about the Big D and Madison—or any subject, for that matter.

"What will you do for the holiday, then?" Dad asked Mom. "I don't think you should have to be alone, Frannie."

Mom quickly said that it didn't matter and the most important thing was for Madison to be happy. Eventually Dad agreed with reluctance.

"We'll leave it up to Madison," he said. "She can decide what *she* wants for Thanksgiving."

Suddenly, from the other side of the porch, Phinnie appeared. Madison smiled at him from afar and then he came over, wiggling. Unfortunately, he wiggled over while making the loudest snorts ever. Madison tried to move backward, but *then* she lost her balance.

The weight shifted in Madison's bag, and the heaviness of all those books sent her toppling. It was her second fall in two days! Madison felt like Queen of the Klutzes.

Phin ran away. And then Dad heard. He leaned into the screen to see Madison lying on the porch.

"Maddie?" he cried out through the screen. "What are you doing out there?"

Madison sat up. "Just hanging out, Dad. What are you doing in there?"

Mom had made her way outside by then. She extended a hand to pull her daughter upright again. She helped Madison pick up her bag, too.

"Hi, Mom," Madison said softly. "What's going on?"

Mom crossed her arms. "Why don't you come inside so we can all talk."

All week, Maddie had worked herself up into a tizzy about the change in family plans for the holiday. But now Madison knew Thanksgiving would *really* never be the same again. Seventh grade was bringing big changes not only at school. It was making bigger-than-big changes at home.

And Madison was right smack-dab in the middle of it all.

Chapter 10

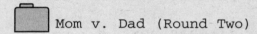 Mom v. Dad (Round Two)

Two weird things about dealing with parents who have had the Big D:

1. When they ask, "What do YOU want?" something is wrong. They don't know what to do. It's better to play dumb.
2. Do not eavesdrop while kneeling (very painful).

Mom and Dad expect ME to decide about Thanksgiving? It seems totally unfair, since they're the grown-ups and I'm the kid. This is like a tug-of-war and I never liked stupid tug-of-war! At second-grade field day we played that game and I fell in the mud.

My head hurts just thinking about all this stuff.

Bigfishbowl.com was busy on Sunday night. Madison went online to find her keypal or maybe even her BFFs. Bigwheels would have something encouraging to say. But Madison ended up in the middle of a three-way chat with Aimee and Fiona instead.

```
<MadFinn>: AIMEE!!!!!!
<BalletGrl>: I found this wicked
    cool ballet chat room I've been
    here like 2 hrs.
<MadFinn>: is Fiona online 2?
<Wetwinz>: hi
<MadFinn>: EGG is sooooooo lame you
    guys
<BalletGrl>: what now
<MadFinn>:  :-< he blew me off
<Wetwinz>: ur ss project? I thought
    u met @ his house
<BalletGrl>: WAI
<Wetwinz>: u guys always say stuff
    about him stop!
<MadFinn>: what did u do today
<Wetwinz>: Dad made the plane
    reservations for Thanksgiving.
    We're leaving a day early so I
    get to miss school that Wed.
    before. California here I come.
<BalletGrl>: you are so lucky
<MadFinn>: I am spending it w/Dad
    now
```

```
<BalletGrl>: ???????
<MadFinn>: and Stephanie. Mom said I
    could.
<Wetwinz>: that's kewl
<MadFinn>: is it weird to leave Mom
    alone though?
<BalletGrl>: Yup I think so YES
<Wetwinz>: maybe
<MadFinn>: I wanna DTRT
<Wetwinz>: Do the right thing! yeah
<BalletGrl>: I have to finish
    homework I've been on the
    computer for a long time bye!
<Wetwinz>: Daisy and I finished our
    extra credit we're doing Pilgrims
<MadFinn>: u guys what should I
    do????
<BalletGrl>: NOTHING ha ha ha ha ha
<BalletGrl>: <k>
<Wetwinz>: peace out
```

Before Madison logged off, her mailbox blinked with three messages.

FROM	SUBJECT
✉ GoGramma	RECIPES
✉ Eggaway	Project
✉ Dantheman	SUGAR

First Madison saw a note with attachments from Gramma Helen in Chicago.

From: GoGramma
To: MadFinn
Subject: RECIPES
Date: Sun 19 Nov 5:28 PM

Hello, there. I miss you very much. But your aunt is taking very good care of me here.

Since you will be spending Thanksgiving with your mother, I thought you might like to make some of my favorite recipes for dinner.

Your uncle here showed me how to attach a file to this message, so I hope that works. Write again and tell me all about your other classes.

The volunteering job sounds like fun, too.

Love, Gramma

<<Attachment: FruitTerrine.doc>>
<<Attachment: GrammaStuffing.doc>>
<<Attachment: SweetPotatoPie.doc>>

The second e-mail was from Egg.

```
From: Eggaway
To: MadFinn
Subject: Project
Date: Sun 19 Nov 5:33 PM
```
U R gonna be so psyched. I added
these noises to the *Mayflower*
presentation. Now when you put the
mouse on the ship, you can hear
seagulls and water noises and surf.
Mariah helped out. Hope that's OK.
BFN.

The final message was from Dan Ginsburg, and he'd marked it high priority.

```
Priority: HIGH
From: Dantheman
To: MadFinn
Subject: SUGAR
Date: Sun 19 Nov 6:09 PM
```
My mom just told me that Sugar was
sick and might need surgery. Will
you be coming to the clinic
tomorrow? I know u said u might
show up. I think Sugar would like
to see a friend. C U in school.

Sugar the schnoodle was sick? The pooch was alone in the world, without a family to love and protect her. Madison knew Dr. Wing was the best

veterinarian in Far Hills, but Madison was sadder than sad about Sugar.

She grabbed her math notebook and plopped down in her plastic purple chair. She wanted to catch up on studying so she'd be able to go to the clinic tomorrow after school. Sugar would need her.

Monday morning Madison was still feeling a little sad. She looked everywhere to find Dan before homeroom, but the halls were too busy to track him down. Science class at the end of the day couldn't come soon enough. She'd see Dan there.

The science lab room was abuzz with chatter. Mr. Danehy wasn't always great at keeping order in the classroom.

Madison heard the whispers but didn't think much of it at first. Then she looked up to find an entire row of kids staring. *Staring* right at her.

Shifting in her chair, Madison tried to act casual. But people were still staring, and she didn't know why.

"Hey, Finnster," Hart said. He was sitting a stool away. "What's the deal?"

Madison was *utterly* perplexed. "The *deal*?"

But Hart didn't answer. This time, it was her lab partner, Poison Ivy Daly, who spoke up.

"Everyone says you and Dan Ginsburg are going out."

"What?" Madison blurted. "Everyone *who*?"

"You know." Ivy snapped her gum. *"Everyone."*

"You're kidding, right?" Madison said. But "everyone" was still staring. And now everyone was talking.

Mr. Danehy smacked his palm on the chalkboard at the front of the room.

"Enough! Silence!" he commanded.

Everyone hushed, even Madison. She was squirming in her seat.

Ivy started to laugh. Then her drones, Rose and Joan, laughed.

Mr. Danehy waved his hand in the air. "Just what is so funny, Miss Daly?"

Ivy sucked her laughs back in. "Nothing, Mr. Danehy."

Madison bowed her head and made a wish that by some magic scientific power, Mr. Danehy would force Ivy out of her chair and out into the hallway.

She looked around.

Had everyone heard Ivy's rumor?

Madison's stomach lurched. Had Hart Jones even heard the gossip? What did her crush think?

"What's the matter, Madison?" Ivy taunted in a low voice from where she was sitting. "You didn't think anyone saw you on your ice cream date? I saw you and your boyfriend, Dan."

Madison looked around the room again. Dan was across the room. He smiled in her direction.

"He's not my boyfriend," Madison snapped. Her

face was red-hot. Embarrassment and anger boiled inside like lava ready to burst. "He's my FRIEND," she said firmly, glaring at Ivy. "Not that YOU know anything about having a real friend."

Ivy didn't answer. She just tossed her head. "Don't get so huffy, Madison."

After class, Madison rushed out the door. She went directly to Mrs. Wing's classroom, where she was supposed to meet Egg.

"Hi," Madison said quietly. "Egg, can I ask you something?"

"Look at *this*!" he showed Madison some of the extra-special effects he'd added to the computer. The cursor was a Pilgrim hat.

"Egg . . . did you hear anything weird lately? About me?" Madison asked.

"Huh? What?" Egg shook his head.

Madison shrugged. "Nothing. I just heard this rumor in science class and . . . well . . . about me and Dan. . . ."

Egg laughed out loud. "Are you joking?"

"So you didn't hear Ivy Daly spreading any rumors?" Madison asked a second time, just to be sure.

"Ivy Daly is a dork," Egg said. "Don't worry about it. No one ever believes her, anyway."

Madison smiled. "Thanks, Egg. I'm really sorry for being upset."

"That's okay," Egg said. "But before we practice, tell me what are we going to say again? You're way better than me at presenting."

The next half hour they reviewed facts and planned who would say what during the presentation. Then they went upstairs to the media center. The librarian, Mr. Books, let Egg print out a few pages with the color laser printer. He'd downloaded pictures of cartoon Pilgrims, and Madison and Egg glued the pictures on their poster of the *Mayflower*.

Their run-through went *perfectly*.

Madison felt very thankful to have Egg as her friend—and social studies partner.

She started a brand-new file when she got home.

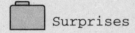 Surprises

Surprises can be awful. Like the Dan gossip. How would Ivy have seen me and Dan having an ice cream cone? But surprises can be good.
1. After a week of yucky work, Egg turned up to meet me and was 100 percent prepared. Our presentation is going to be the BEST. He has special effects on the computer. He's so good at that stuff. He even added MUSIC! We worked on the construction of the paper Mayflower together. I did lots of the work on that—even added glitter glue even if it's not a real Pilgrim kind of thing.

2. Sugar doesn't need surgery! Dan called to tell me that she is just going through shock or something after being rescued. I can't wait to see her this week.

Any day now I'm expecting some kind of a surprise from Mom and Dad. They are mostly acting cool around me, but I don't know. How do they really feel about me going with Dad? Am I hurting Mom's feelings by picking him? Are they going to start all that arguing again?

There is still something not right about the whole thing. Life after the big D is one surprise I can never seem to figure out.

Chapter 11

When Madison's alarm went off, she stayed under the covers. Her insides felt fluttery, like she was on a ride at the amusement park. She definitely didn't want to risk eating breakfast.

Today were the extra-credit presentations.

She hoped that Egg wouldn't be late . . . or forget. She wondered if Egg was nervous right now, too.

"It's almost eight!" Mom yelled from downstairs. "You better be out of that bed!"

Madison leaped up. "Drat! Drat!"

Now she was *late*.

Rushing around wasn't the way Madison had hoped to spend the morning before her presentation. But here she was, frantically pulling on socks and sneakers and combing her hair. Even more ominous was the rain that started to pour outside. She tied her hair back into a ponytail to avoid a bad case of the frizzies.

"You're going to do fine," Mom reassured her. "I'll drive you over to school today. The rain looks very bad."

The car ride made Madison a little queasy. The orange juice Mom had made her drink was sloshing inside her empty tummy. Mom told her to take deep breaths and to relax.

Madison arrived at school a little damp, but on time. But Egg wasn't there.

All through homeroom, Madison watched the door. But no Egg.

Egg still hadn't appeared at the end of homeroom. Madison thought maybe he would go straight to Mrs. Belden's classroom.

Madison sat down next to Fiona and Daisy. They looked so funny because they had dressed up in "period" costumes. Daisy wore a ratty-looking black beard and a cardboard top hat she'd obviously stapled together quickly with black construction paper. Fiona wore her hair in two braids on either side of her head.

"So you guys are Abe Lincoln and *who*?" Aimee asked them.

"You'll see," Fiona said, acting mysterious. "I can't believe you forgot already. I told you last week."

"What is the soccer ball for?" Ben the brainiac asked.

"Oh," Daisy said. "The ball is just from morning practice. I forgot to put it into my locker."

"Ohhhh," Ben rolled his eyes.

"What's your report on?" Daisy asked Ben and Aimee.

"We're doing a report on Native Americans," Ben said.

"Wampanoog," Aimee added.

"Wampanoag," he corrected her. "Sounds like frog. You better get it right in class."

Aimee laughed. "You better not tell me what to do, Ben." She tapped his shoulder and tossed her hair a little.

Ben turned pink. "Uh-huh."

Madison chuckled. Maybe Aimee really did have a crush on Ben.

Once more, Madison searched the halls for Egg, but he was still nowhere to be seen.

Madison's stomach was doing super-duper loop de loops. In thirty seconds the bell was going to ring. *Where was Egg?*

Madison knew that Mrs. Belden always shut the door tight and didn't approve of latecomers. Her skin felt all clammy with the anticipation. First she had been rushing. Now she was waiting.

"Are you okay?" Poison Ivy said to Madison. "You look a little sick. Is that sweat?"

Madison wiped her brow with one sleeve and pursed her lips. "Did you say something?" she said to Ivy. Madison was in no mood for Ivy's poisonous comments today.

Ivy turned back to Drew. "What's her problem?" she asked him. But Drew didn't say a word.

Madison looked at the clock. "Do you know where Egg is?" she whispered to Drew.

"No, I dunno where he is."

Brrrrrrring!

"Looks like someone has a problem," Ivy taunted. Her drones giggled from a few rows back.

Madison shot Ivy a glare. "Looks like you're the one with a problem, Ivy," she whispered back to her enemy.

Drew laughed. Ivy was speechless.

Madison watched the classroom door. Mrs. Belden was about to close it. She had her fingers on the knob, even. But then Egg appeared!

Mrs. Belden grinned and motioned Madison over.

"What happened to you?" Madison whispered to Egg. He pulled her aside, and Madison expected to hear a long list of reasons why Egg was later than late. She expected to hear: "The entire project got mangled and I was trying to re-sort it on my computer," or, "I deleted the *Mayflower* program by mistake," or, "I'm sick as a dog and I don't want to do this."

But that wasn't what Egg said at all.

"I'm sorry, Maddie. I was just nervous. I wanted to check the whole program again just to make sure it worked, so I went up to the media center and . . ."

"Forget about it," Madison said. "We're good to go."

Madison could feel her heart beating. For whatever reason, the simple extra-credit report had become all-important for Madison. This was about more than the *Mayflower* and grades. This was about her and Egg working together.

"Hey, Maddie," Egg whispered. "I gotta show you something."

Egg showed her the giant, color poster of the *Mayflower* they had made together. Egg had pasted more smaller pictures and labels onto the different areas Madison had laid out. She'd talked about adding more detail, but they hadn't had enough time.

"What is THAT?" Madison asked.

"I added more stuff, like you wanted."

"Wow." Madison was stunned. She hadn't even known he was paying attention to anything she'd said the whole time they'd been working together on the project. "You did all that last night?"

"I know you wanted this to be really special. Besides, my sister helped me."

Madison was happier than happy. "It is so cool."

"I think you were right about having something to pass around and show in class. And I have my

117

laptop inside all ready for the PowerPoint," Egg said.

Mrs. Belden stuck her head out into the hallway. "Why don't you two go first so you can pass out your materials and then sit down to watch the others."

Egg and Madison walked into the class with the homemade *and* computerized *Mayflower*s. Ivy was staring. Rose was staring. Drew was staring. *Everyone* had all eyes on them. Going first was the worst. Madison could feel her heart thump. But this kind of staring was different than in science class. This was the good kind. Egg handed out the fact sheets Madison had typed up.

"Should I start?" she nervously asked.

Mrs. Belden nodded.

Madison's dad told her she should begin the presentation with a joke. Madison knew the perfect one.

"If April showers bring May flowers, what do *May flowers* bring?"

"Pilgrims!" Dan shouted from the back.

"Like we don't all know that joke already." Ivy grunted. "Come on."

"Miss Daly, that is unnecessary," Mrs. Belden said.

Ivy crossed her legs with a huff. "Sorry."

Madison continued. "Egg and I have created a model of the *Mayflower*, a ship that brought the Pilgrims to the New World. We found out some interesting facts about the *Mayflower*."

"There were lots of trading ships at the time that were also called the *Mayflower*," Egg said.

"And this ship wasn't meant to carry passengers," Madison added. "Originally. But people squeezed into the area with livestock and guns in between decks."

Everyone gathered around the computer while Egg and Madison explained. It took a little longer than five minutes, but Mrs. Belden seemed very impressed.

"That was an excellent example of teamwork," she told the class. "You two get a gold star for organization."

Madison and Egg beamed. They had been greater-than-great partners, better than expected. Madison had worried for nothing. Egg had come through! After some polite applause, they sat down on the side of the room. Aimee leaned over and whispered, "Way to go." Fiona smiled at Madison, too. She was proud.

Fiona and Daisy presented next. Unfortunately, their extra-credit project had a few loose ends—and nothing seemed to work out right. Fiona's costume ripped, Daisy lost her place *six* times while reading the Thanksgiving Proclamation, and they sometimes talked so quickly that no one could understand a single word.

But Mrs. Belden was generous with her compliments. "Very creative, girls," she said when they sat down again. "I like the costumes and the narration of Sarah Hale, Fiona."

Fiona sank into her seat again, eyes on the floor.

Aimee and Ben gave the most embarrassing presentation of the morning. Aimee looked a little lost, which was very unlike the dancing, showy presenter she could be. Madison wondered if maybe, just maybe, Aimee's crushing on Ben was the reason. Madison was getting pretty good at crush detecting. She'd never seen Aimee so distracted by someone.

Mrs. Belden had to cut off Ben when he talked for too long about Samoset and Squanto, the Native Americans who had helped the Pilgrims in Plymouth. Aimee stood by, flashing pictures and maps.

"Well done," Mrs. Belden interrupted. "I think we all agree that was quite a history lesson, Ben and Aimee."

As soon as they were finished, Poison Ivy and Drew were called up to present their extra credit. Both Drew and Ivy were dressed like Pilgrims. Ivy passed around a basket with corn bread in it and talked about how women Pilgrims had no say but did all the work. She even claimed to be a direct descendant of Pilgrims on the *Mayflower*.

"You never told me that," Drew suddenly blurted.

"Shhh," Ivy hissed, and kept right on talking.

Mrs. Belden interrupted. "Is this true, Ivy? That's a big thing."

"Ummm . . . well . . . not really. But aren't we all related? I mean, what's the big deal?"

The class got very quiet. Ivy shifted from foot to foot. Drew had a blank stare on his face.

Mrs. Belden spoke up. "Please continue, Ivy."

But she didn't say a word. Poison Ivy Daly looked like she was about to hyperventilate.

Some kid in the back of the classroom moved, and his chair squeaked. That's when Drew started to laugh. It wasn't a teeny giggle, but a big snorting laugh. And it was supercontagious.

Even Mrs. Belden had to cover her mouth so she wouldn't laugh.

Ivy glanced around the room. "May I please be excused?" she asked, and ran out into the hall.

A few moments later, Ivy returned to class with Mrs. Belden. She looked like she was sniffling, but her lip gloss looked perfect. When Ivy walked past Madison to go back to her seat, Madison couldn't help but smile a little. It served her right for starting a rumor about her and Dan. Being in the spotlight wasn't always so great—even for Ivy Daly.

Then Dan and Hart were the next ones up to present.

Once they reached the front of the classroom, both boys slipped trash bags over their bodies with a cutout hole for their heads. The bags had colored paper feathers, and they each wore backward baseball caps with more feathers taped to the brims.

"Today we would like to do our extra-credit project to a song," Hart joked.

Everyone snickered.

"Yeah," Dan continued. "Called 'The Turkey Pokey.'"

Everyone laughed out LOUD.

"You put your right wing in, you put your left wing out, you do the turkey pokey and you turn yourself around." It was sung to the tune of the regular "Hokey Pokey." Mrs. Belden was smiling to herself the whole time the boys were singing.

The turkey getup was Dan's idea. He wanted to celebrate the bird that—in his words—"got wicked gypped every Thanksgiving." Dan had a true animal-lover side to his personality. Meanwhile Hart decided it would be funny to dress up and "talk turkey," too. They presented random facts about turkey symbolism and turkeys from other cultures and explained how Native Americans turned turkey feathers into beautiful cloaks.

"This was a highly original presentation, boys," Mrs. Belden said as the bell rang. Extra credit had been a lot more fun than anyone expected.

That night, Madison sent Egg an e-mail message.

```
From: MadFinn
To: Eggaway
Subject: MAYFLOWER PRESENTATION
Date: Tues 21 Nov 4:52 PM
We had the best presentation. You
are so awesome and I am soooooo
sorry for not believing we could do
```

it. Thanks 4 all ur work, Egg. BTW:
my mom says she wants to see it
sometime, so maybe you can come
over? I hope we r still good
friends. TTFN. <:>== (p.s. That's a
symbol for a turkey ha ha!!)

Madison noticed she had another e-mail in the box. It was from Dad, and he'd sent it to Stephanie, too. It looked serious.

From: JeffFinn
To: MadFinn
Cc: Stephie8
Subject: Thanksgiving Feast
Date: Tues 21 Nov 5:02 PM

Maddie, I wanted to call to talk to
you, but the phone has been busy,
so I sent this instead. We need to
talk about Thanksgiving again. I
want to make sure you know
everything because we have some big
plans. Things have changed a little.
But I know you will love it.

Stephanie's family has kindly
extended an invitation to their home
in Texas, and I would like to go
with her and bring you along. Isn't
that exciting? You've never been to
Texas before! What do you think? We

would have so much fun. Stephanie
has an enormous family with lots of
kids your age.

Call me soon so we can talk. I love
you!

Madison reread the e-mail and caught her
breath. No, she'd never been to Texas before. And
she didn't want to go now.
She didn't want to go *ever*.

Chapter 12

"Time for school," Mom said, tugging the comforter off Madison's bed.

"No," Madison said, curling back into her pillows.

Mom sat on the edge of the bed. "Would you please talk to me? What is going on?"

Madison hadn't said anything last night to Mom about Thanksgiving because she figured Dad would. But Dad probably knew Mom wasn't going to like the arrangement one bit.

Thanksgiving was tomorrow. It was enough to make someone want to stay under the covers forever.

How would Madison break the news to Mom about Texas?

"Mom," Madison said quietly. "Can we talk?"

Mom frowned. "Is something wrong, honey

bear? Are you sick? You haven't really been yourself for the last—"

"I don't want to spend Thanksgiving with Dad!" Madison blurted.

Mom leaned backward with a quizzical look on her face. "We've been through this already, Maddie. It's really okay with me. I understand. Being in this house will be hard over the holiday."

"You don't get it, Mom," Madison insisted.

"What don't I get?"

"Spending Thanksgiving with Dad doesn't mean being with him only. It means spending it with Stephanie, too."

Mom stroked Madison's forehead. "You like her, Maddie. She's a nice person."

"You still don't get it. It means being with Stephanie and everyone in her family. And I don't want Thanksgiving with her family, and that's where Dad's going. He wants me to fly to Texas to be with him. Ugh."

This was definitely news to Mom. But she kept her cool.

"I see." Mom nodded. "Well, Maddie, I think Dad is trying to make you feel included. And I think Stephanie has a big family. Dad probably thought you'd enjoy an adventure. You were very vocal about not wanting to stay in this house or even in Far Hills. Remember?"

Madison nodded. She was the one who had

started the Thanksgiving tug-of-war. Madison had made such a big deal, and now here she was going back to the original plan.

"Have you told your father how you feel?" Mom asked.

"Not exactly," Madison shrugged. "He'll be mad at me."

Mom laughed. "Maddie, your dad won't get mad at you. I think you need to call him. Come on. We have time before school. You need to do this now."

Madison dialed Dad's house.

Dad was silent at first, and Madison got worried about what he might say next.

"I'm sorry, sweetheart," he finally said. "I had no intention of putting you in the middle of this. I guess we just all want to be with you. I think you should stay at home with Mom, and I'll see you when we get back. How does that sound?"

Madison felt warm all over. Once again, Dad had said exactly the right thing to make her feel better.

When she hung up the phone, Mom leaned in for a giant hug.

"So does this mean it's just you and me again?" Mom asked.

Madison just smiled.

The day was a lot brighter. And it wasn't just that the rain had stopped. Madison hadn't realized just how much the whole Thanksgiving decision-making process had been clouding her days. Now that things were settled, she was feeling much better.

On the way to her first class, she caught a glimpse of herself in a display cabinet outside the history department. She smoothed her ponytail down in the glass reflection.

It took her a few moments before she even noticed the display on Thanksgiving. Around the borders of the glass window were acorns and pumpkins. Different teachers had posted artwork and papers. But in the center of the entire display was the *Mayflower* poster Madison and Egg had created together.

There she was—right there in the middle of everything. Extra credit turned into extra recognition. Madison felt really proud.

The second bell rang, and Madison caught up with Aimee and Fiona. "Where have you been?" Aimee asked. "I looked for you on the way to school. You haven't been walking much this week, have you?"

"Mom gave me a ride again," Madison said. She didn't feel like going into more detail about Thanksgiving and Mom and Dad and everything else that got messed up. Aimee didn't ask any more questions.

Later in the day, Mom surprised Madison by picking her up and driving over to the clinic. Dan hitched a ride with them, too.

Eileen was busy working at the front desk in a new T-shirt that read BE A VEGETARIAN.

Madison and Dan went into the paneled office and entered data into the database. Then they joined Eileen and a few other volunteers to hang special decorations. Madison hung up one poster that read SAVE THE TURKEYS. Eileen even hung up a funny turkey mobile with a moving turkey wattle (the icky red jiggly thing under a turkey's chin).

"I saw a wild turkey last week," Dan said as he hung up a turkey poster. "It was so big. I wonder if someone got him for the holiday?"

"You mean . . . ate him?" Madison laughed.

They both made an "eeeeeew" noise and laughed some more.

"I am so glad I came to volunteer here, Dan," Madison said. "I know that sounds really sappy, but I am. And I'm glad we got to be better friends."

"Yeah," Dan said. "It's been cool having you around. The animals really like you."

"Thanks." Madison reached out and petted Sugar's paw. it was dangling out of her cage. "Is that what you think, Sugar?"

The schnoodle made a low noise that Madison took as a qualified "yes" to her question.

Dan grabbed a few leashes off the Peg-Board at the side of the room.

"Hey," he said, tossing a leash to Madison. "Let's take her for a walk. I'll get some of the others."

Madison put on her scarf and her jacket. She gently lifted Sugar out of a cage and hooked on her leash. Dan let out some of the other animals, too: the yellow Labrador retriever, a miniature dachshund, a Jack Russell terrier, and a Yorkie terrier.

They walked up and down in front of the clinic a few times and then crossed over to walk on the other side of the street.

"HELP!" Madison laughed as the dogs swarmed around her. The leashes were getting tangled quickly.

Dan laughed, too. "This would make a funny picture."

"Good thing no one has a camera," Madison said.

They walked around the block. Dan wasn't talking too much. Madison didn't know why.

"What do you guys do for Thanksgiving?" Madison asked.

He shrugged. "You mean me and my mom?"

"Yeah," Madison said.

"This is a weird time of year. My dad died around this time two years ago."

Madison was amazed at how honest Dan was being, like they'd been friends forever and ever.

She took a breath. "I'm so sorry."

"Yeah, me too." Dan smiled. "He was a cool guy."

"Did he like animals, too?" Madison asked, leaning down to pet the top of Sugar's head.

Dan thought for a minute. "Yeah, I guess so. We always had pets. I remember this duck that lived in our yard."

Madison wanted to ask more questions about Dan's dad, but she didn't know how. She started asking about his mom instead.

"Your mom is so cool," Madison said. "Especially the T-shirts she wears."

"Yeah," Dan said. "She has a ton of them, right?"

When they walked back inside the clinic from exercising the dogs, Eileen was hanging a red-and-orange streamer across the waiting area. It really brightened up the place.

Madison packed up her stuff and wished Dan and his mom a happy holiday. Her own mom was waiting in the car outside.

That night, Madison wrote a quick e-mail to Dan, thanking him for being so nice at the clinic. It was Thanksgiving, after all. She figured that was a good thing to do. Madison found some other e-mails waiting for her.

FROM	SUBJECT
✉ Wetwinz	We're Here!!!!
✉ Bigwheels	Turkeys

One was from Fiona. She had left that morning on a flight to California.

From: Wetwinz
To: MadFinn, BalletGrl
Subject: We're here!!!!
Date: Wed 22 Nov 1:11 PM

I miss u guys already! Boo hoo. Our flight was totally packed with kids. I babysat a little for this one woman's little girl. She was sooooo adorable.

Oh no, I left my favorite dress @ home but NBD, I'll live, I guess. Mom said maybe we can shop today for something new.

It's not that warm here like beach weather, but the sun is shining and it's way different than Far Hills. I've already seen my BFF from here and I ran into this old boyfriend who is a year older. His name is Julio. You would freak, he is so cute. He has a new girlfriend, though—oh, well.

N e way, I am going with Chet to the mall and we're hanging with his old crowd of friends. I wish you guys could be here. I hope you have a happy Thanksgiving. . . .

Love and smooches fm. me! Xoxoxoox

p.s. Howz Egg? LOL say hello to him & Drew 4 me.

p.p.s. Let's go to bigfishbowl and IM each other soon.

Madison grinned at the screen and pressed SAVE. That message was a keeper. She was just as thrilled to see a short and sweet note from Bigwheels, too.

From: Bigwheels
To: MadFinn
Subject: Turkeys
Date: Wed 22 Nov 11:52 AM
Long time, no write? I know you've been busy, but I miss our notes. Please send news about anything. Have you ever heard this quote: If you want to soar with the eagles, you have to put up with a lot of turkeys. LOL.

I thought you or your dad would like that one.

We're having dinner with both sets of grandparents, my parents, my sister and brother, and loads of aunts and uncles and cousins. I think I told you. Anyway, I'm nervous to see some of my other cousins because they can be really snotty to me. I don't know why. I would never treat someone that way. Would you?

Thanks for being my friend at Thanksgiving!

Yours till the potatoes mash,

Bigwheels

After reading both e-mails three times each, Madison went immediately into her files. She had started the year unsure about her friends, but here they were all around her. It was ridiculous to think that she had a whole lot of thanks for *nothing*. Right now, her life was chock-full as Madison's kindergarten cornucopia Mom had displayed atop the mantel. She was bursting.

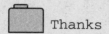 Thanks

Rude Awakening: Good things are like grapes. They come in bunches.

I had a long talk with Dad today about spending Thanksgiving with Mom. He was very cool about it. So now I am actually looking forward to being alone together. I don't need a million people around to eat turkey.

Mom and I are going to make the pie and stuffing tomorrow. No more surprises!

Things couldn't be yummier.

Chapter 13

Madison rolled over and opened her eyes, thinking it was later than it was. Outside was still dark, just beginning to lighten up. The trees were moving in the wind outside her window.

She sat up and put on slippers and shuffled down the hall to her mother's bedroom. Phinnie was sprawled on top of Mom's bed, eyes glistening in the half dark. She climbed up and kissed Mom's cheek.

"Happy Thanksgiving, Mom," Madison said.

Bleary-eyed, Mom awoke with a start. "Maddie, you scared me half to death. I was in the middle of a dream."

They lay in bed and talked about Mom's dream and about Thanksgivings long ago, like the time when Mom had to be rushed to the emergency room for slicing her finger while cooking.

"I remember that was really gross," Madison said. "There was blood all over the counter."

"It always looks worse than it is," Mom said. She smiled all of a sudden, and Madison felt self-conscious.

"What? What are you looking at?" Madison said.

"You. You look so pretty in this light."

Madison made a face. "You mean I look pretty in the dark?"

They laughed and got out of bed.

Mom spent the morning speaking with international clients as she'd been doing all week. They faxed notes to her and important contracts. Mom's latest project for Budge Films was taking up so much time. Madison wondered why anyone would have to work on Thanksgiving since it was a holiday. Then she remembered that it was only a holiday in America, so everyone else in the world had to show up at work the usual time and place.

Madison figured she'd get a head start working on dinner in the kitchen. She took out the peeler and started peeling carrots into a big bowl. She made a feeble attempt at skinning the sweet potatoes, too, but they were so tough and hard to peel. She needed Mom's help for those.

While Mom worked, Madison also watched some television, like the Macy's Thanksgiving parade. When she had been younger, Mom and Dad would sometimes take her into New York City to watch people blow up the giant balloons and floats on the night before the parade started. It was magic to see Big Bird and Spiderman get inflated into enormous, building-sized balloons.

Today Madison watched the balloons on TV only. She curled up into a little ball under Gramma's afghan on the sofa and counted the number of baton twirlers in every marching band. Next year, Madison would have to ask to go back to the city and watch the parade in person. She didn't think Mom would go for it, but it couldn't hurt to ask.

As she was lying on the sofa, Phinnie walked by Madison. She called out for him to come over and snuzzle, but he walked right on by. *Again.* Now Madison was starting to take it personally. Or maybe the dog was sick? She worried a little, but not enough to get up and take Phin's temperature or pet his little nose to see if it was warm when it was supposed to be cold and wet. Instead Madison curled deeper into the couch pillows.

Mom came back into the living room after noontime and announced that her work was completed.

"Let's call your gramma!" she suggested, grabbing the phone and squeezing in next to Madison on the couch. They dialed the number.

"Hello, there." Gramma's voice came across loud and clear.

"Hey, Mother," Mom said. "It's me and Maddie. We called to say hello. How's the turkey in Chicago?"

"Turkey's been in the oven since seven. Angie and Bob are coming over later today."

"Mother, I really am sorry we couldn't make it there. We miss you."

When it was her turn to speak, Madison grabbed the phone from her mom and shouted into the receiver. "Warm hugs from me, Gramma," Madison said. "And Phinnie, too."

Gramma chuckled. "What did you say, dear?" she asked. Madison realized she'd taken out her hearing aid. "You're finished with who?"

"Oh, nothing, Gramma. We made all your recipes today. Thank you for them. The stuffing is yummy."

"That's fantastic. Well, I love you, Maddie, dear," Gramma said. "Did you hear me?"

"Loud and clear," Madison said. "Let me put Mom back on the phone, okay?"

No sooner had the call to Chicago ended than the phone rang again. Madison hoped inside her heart when she picked up the phone that it would be a certain person—and it was.

"DADDY!" she screeched into the receiver.

He was gushing all over the place about missing Madison. He told her that Texas just wasn't the same without her. The night before, he and Stephanie had been to a steer auction near the family ranch.

"Stephanie lived on a ranch?" Madison asked.

"Yup," Dad said. "I am now an official cowboy, so watch out."

Madison laughed.

"Honey, Stephanie was here a moment ago," Dad continued. "She wanted me to wish you a happy Thanksgiving, okay?"

Madison felt a twinge of sadness because good-byes with Dad were always the hardest, no matter where she was or what she was doing. Even on the telephone.

With family phone calls out of the way, the dinner preparations started for real around one o'clock. All the vegetables—including sweet potatoes—had been peeled. Madison had mixed the stuffing's dry ingredients into a bowl. Mom came along and helped pull everything together the best she could.

Mom wasn't a great cook, but she didn't mind experimenting. Mostly, she was a bad cook not because she was untalented—it was more like she was too busy. Her job took up so much of her time.

An hour into the cooking frenzy, everything seemed to be going along great. The food was all cooking inside the oven, and Madison and Mom went into the den to watch a little more television.

As soon as Mom and Madison snuggled into the couch, the kitchen smoke alarm went off and they both jumped clear out of their seats. The small drippings from Gramma's sweet potato pie had set off a burnt, smoky bomb inside the kitchen. The whole kitchen smelled like burning sugar, a funny, sweet smell that made Madison a little queasy.

139

"The pie is ruined," Madison said as she carefully pulled on pot holders and rested it on a pie sheet. It was all black and burned around the edges, but Mom set it aside for a special dessert anyhow.

Dingdong.

Madison turned around toward the kitchen sliding door. Aimee was standing outside with a wrapped package, twirling around. "Brrrrrrr!" she said as Madison pulled open the sliding door. "Happy Nonturkey Day!"

Mom laughed.

"You're still in your pajamas!" Aimee gasped. "I had to get ready early because people were coming over."

"We're just hanging out," Madison said, catching the corner of Mom's eye.

"You are so lucky, Maddie. I wish I could have a mellow Thanksgiving like you. I have to be stuck at home with my dumb brothers, who are so annoying," Aimee wailed. "All they do is watch football."

"I like football," Madison said.

"Then you hang out with them. I just want to go to the movies or something," Aimee said. She put a small tinfoil package up on the countertop. "My mom said to give you guys this. It's a loaf of her macrobiotic apple bread. It's made with honey and oats or something."

"That's very nice, Aimee. Thank your mom for us both."

"Well, back to my family!" Aimee announced with flair. She twirled her arms into the air. "Ta da! Now you see me, now you—"

She jumped back out the same way she came.

"Call me later!" Aimee yelled through the glass sliding door. She made a goofy face and vanished.

Dinner was half burnt and half cold, but *all* fun. Madison and Mom couldn't believe that they had actually made any meal as elaborate as Thanksgiving dinner, complete with a Jell-O mold and a bowl of homemade stuffing.

"Does this taste funny to you?" Madison asked when she took a bite of stuffing.

Mom grinned. "Probably." She took a pinch of the stuffing and put it under the table. "Here, Phinnie! Mom has something for you."

They both burst into laughter.

Dessert, they decided, would be saved for later in the evening. Mom said they'd have some time to digest first. She seemed to have a plan about the whole day. Together they washed up the dishes and played a game of Scrabble.

Around seven-thirty, the doorbell rang.

"Who could that be?" Mom asked.

Madison shrugged. She had no clue. "Maybe it's Aimee again? Or Egg?"

Dingdong.

It rang a second time, and neither Mom nor Madison moved.

141

"Are you going to get it?" Mom asked.

Madison begrudgingly got up. She looked down at herself. She hadn't changed out of her pajamas since the morning. She looked like a mess.

"Mom, if it's a boy . . . even just Egg . . . I can't let him see me. . . ."

Mom grinned. "Okay, I'll get the door."

Madison rushed into the small half bathroom downstairs to see what she looked like *exactly*. Her hair was looking a little flyaway, but her pj's looked surprisingly presentable. Only the bear claw slippers that Madison had on her feet looked ridiculous.

"Who is it, Mom?" Madison said as she walked back into the living room.

Madison screamed. "Oh, wow!"

Standing in the doorway was a bunch of orange Mylar balloons with art of cartoon turkeys on each one. Through the balloons, a strange man peeked at Madison and grinned.

"Special delivery for Madison Finn," he said.

Madison squealed. "That's me!"

Mom helped Madsion grab the balloon bunch from the man and signed for them. Madison laughed when she saw what the deliveryman looked like. He was wearing a turkey costume!

Phin loved the balloons even more than Madison. He started running around the house. He even slammed into the side of the chairs as he skidded down the hallway. He was that excited.

142

"Rowrooooo!" he yelped.

"Read the card," Mom said, pulling the small blue envelope from the bunch of balloon strings.

Madison opened the card so fast, it almost ripped.

> For Maddie
> With love and drumsticks
> From Dad and Stephanie

"Isn't that nice," Mom said.

Madison nodded. "This whole Thanksgiving is nice, Mom."

Mom disappeared into the kitchen and brought out a big tray with Gramma Helen's sweet potato pie, milk, tea, and some cookies, too.

"The pie looks a little crispy," Madison said. It was scorched around the edges.

"Well, I'm not a super cook yet, but I'm working on it, honey bear," Mom said. "We can cut around the burned parts."

Madison smiled. She had made the right decision about Thanksgiving. She *could* have her turkey and pie *and* eat it, too. And surprises never seemed to end. . . .

Chapter 14

The next morning Madison was so hungry, she took a bite of cold sweet potato pie before she even had breakfast.

She could barely wait to tell Aimee about every-thing that had happened, but Aimee and her broth-ers weren't around, so she left a voice message to call back. Aimee was probably over at her father's bookstore, Book Web.

Madison got ready for the clinic. Mom said that she could spend the day there.

Sugar the schnoodle was waiting!

Eileen was busy working on some files and paper-work at the front of the clinic when Madison walked in with a spring in her step.

"Hiya!" She waved. Eileen just nodded back a

silent hello. Today her T-shirt said HAVE YOU HUGGED YOUR DOG TODAY?

Hugging Phin was one of Madison's favorite things. And she'd been thinking about hugging Sugar all morning long, too.

Dan wasn't around today. Madison remembered that he had gone for the weekend to his cousin's place in Connecticut. He wouldn't be back until after school break was over.

The only person in the back was Dr. Wing. He was standing in front of the cages.

"Hi!" Madison said as she bounced into the room.

Dr. Wing smiled. "Happy day-after-Thanksgiving. Aren't we chipper?"

"TOTALLY!" Madison said. She went immediately to Sugar's cage. "Is it okay if I walk—hey—wait a minute—"

Madison looked into every cage.

"Sugar? Where's the schnoodle? Oh no, please don't tell me she's sick again!"

Dr. Wing shook his head. "No, nothing like that."

"Where is she?" Madison asked. "Where's Sugar?"

"A nice family from the east side of Far Hills came in and adopted her," the doctor explained. "They'd been considering it, and I guess they made a final decision over the holiday. Isn't that great?"

Madison froze.

All the giddiness that had been swirling inside turned to pure defeat.

Sugar was gone?

"Madison," Dr. Wing said. "What's wrong?"

She shook her head. "I just didn't expect this. Not today."

"Well, it's a great thing. Sugar was a very sad puppy, and now she has a loving, caring family. If that isn't the Thanksgiving spirit, I don't know what is," he said.

"I know, but—" Madison wanted to cry, but she took a deep breath. "It's a surprise, that's all."

"I'm sure Sugar will be very happy with her new family arrangements, Madison. Don't worry."

She had to admit that Sugar being adopted was a good thing. Many times abused and neglected dogs with scars and personality problems had hard times finding new homes. That's what Eileen and Dan had said. Madison wanted Sugar to have a happy home forever.

But it was still hard looking at Sugar's empty cage.

She hadn't even had a chance to say good-bye.

"She is gone now," Mr. Wollensky said. He was there to volunteer today, too. "You look very sad, Madison."

Madison sighed. "I just didn't expect to come here and find her gone like this."

"Is hard to let go, yes?" Mr. Wollensky asked.

Madison watched as he opened up the cage and took out the messy newspapers that were lying across the bottom. Madision watched as Mr. Wollensky cleaned away the only things that were left from Sugar's stay at Far Hills Clinic. Bit by bit, all traces of her were taken away.

Now Madison *really* wanted to cry.

"You feel Sugar in *here*, yes?" Mr. Wollensky pointed to his heart. Madison felt a lump in her throat. She did feel Sugar. She missed the schnoodle so much that she couldn't even find the words to describe it. It was an ache—inside.

"Once I had a dog here I wanted to adopt for my own."

"Like Sugar?" Madison said. She had wished that the schnoodle could have been her dog. "What happened?" Madison asked.

"It was not meant to be. This dog ended up with family who could take good care of him. Family's very important."

Madison nodded. She understood. Sugar had a family now, and family, no matter how big or small, was important. Madison thanked Mr. Wollensky and grabbed her coat.

Madison decided to walk home, even though it was a very long walk. A woman across the road was walking a dog that looked familiar. She approached the woman and bent down to pet the dog.

"He's a pug," the woman said. "I hate it when kids call him Squashed-Up Nose and things like that."

Madison smiled. "I know. I have a pug, too."

Suddenly it hit her: she had a pug, too. She already had a dog who she loved more than anything in the whole wide world. And he wasn't going *anywhere*. Madison realized that she hadn't walked Phin in days.

She needed to see Phin—now. She needed to pet his coarse fur, hear his little snuffle, and watch his curlicue tail wiggle.

Soon she was running down the block, running toward home. She'd left her gloves in her orange bag, so her fingertips were like icicles. But she ran faster until she reached the porch at home.

"Phinnie!" Madison gasped a little as she walked back into the house. "Phinnie, where are you?"

Mom appeared in the doorway. "What's going on? I thought you were over at the clinic. You were going to call me to come pick you up. . . ."

Madison was looking all over the front hall. "Mom, where's Phin? Have you seen him? I need to see Phin."

"Hold it, hold it. Shhhhh. Follow me." Mom tiptoed into the den. There, on the den couch, Phin had curled into the tightest ball and was snoring away.

Madison watched him quietly for a few

moments, but then she couldn't contain herself. "Phinnie!" Madison yelled.

He awoke with a snort, and she threw herself over his little pug body.

"Roowwrorooooo!" he yelped right back at her.

Madison lifted Phin into her arms like a baby and carried him upstairs into her bedroom.

"I missed you sooooo much," she cooed in Phin's ears. He licked the tip of her nose and panted. Madison didn't even mind his doggy breath.

With Phin still in her lap, Madison logged on to her laptop computer. She had a special destination in mind, a place she'd discovered a long time ago. Madison plugged a few words into the bigfishbowl search engine, and up popped the address she was looking for.

<u>**Dog**</u> of the Day—Sign Yours Up Now
Tell us about your special **dog**. Is your bichon frise funny? Does your weimaraner whine? Winners daily!

She accessed her photo files and pulled up her favorite shot of Phin. She'd taken it last summer in the backyard. He was standing in tall grass, and the sunlight was hitting his back in just the right places.

"Rowwwroooo!" Phin pushed his snorty nose into her side and wiggled back and forth. He knew how cute he looked.

Madison filled in the Web site form with her dog's full name, Phineas T. Finn, and a few lines about why she loved him.

Phin doesn't mind my messy room. He loves me when I'm sad or happy. And he gives the best hugs in the world. Some people say he looks funny, but I don't think so. Phin is a true member of my family.

Almost immediately, Madison got a return e-mail to inform her that the Dog of the Day submission had been received and would be processed.

"You're my family, Phinnie!" Madison kissed his little ears, and he squirmed. Sooner than soon, he would be making his big Web debut.

Madison opened a blank e-mail and started to write a note to Gramma. She wondered if their Thanksgiving dinner had turned out as nicely as hers had turned out with Mom.

From: MadFinn
To: GoGramma
Subject: I MISS YOU!!!
Date: Fri 24 Nov 1:13 PM
Your sweet potato pie recipe was awesome, Gramma, even if we did burn it a little. Thank you for that. Of course I missed you more

than anything. I had no one to play Crazy Eights with me.

I got a good extra-credit grade in social studies. The teacher gave me and Egg both an A+. She said that we were great partners. I was so nervous, but it's funny how things work out.

I was afraid that if Thanksgiving wasn't the way it always had been that I would be so sad. But change was okay. In the end it was A-okay. Our family is still here. I'm still here, too.

I hope I do get to visit you soon. Mom says maybe she'll let me go to Chicago next summer. I will keep my fingers crossed so I can go.

Thanks for being the best gramma in the universe. Thanks for listening. Thanks for *everything*.

Yours till the pumpkin pies,

Maddie

xoxox

Madison hit SEND. The message went *poof*. As Madison logged off the laptop, Phin jumped off her lap and onto her bed.

"I'll be right back, Phinnie," Madison said, getting up and tiptoeing out of the room. She found Mom downstairs at her own computer.

"Mom?" Madison said as she came into the room. She assumed Mom was doing something work related.

"Come take a look at this, Maddie," Mom said with a big grin.

Madison went over to the desk, and without even thinking, she sat right in Mom's lap. She hadn't sat there in years. It felt good to sit there again.

On the monitor, Madison saw that Mom had made a collage of different photographs from their family. There was a picture of Madison as a little baby. There was a shot of Madison, Mom, and Dad holding a stuffed turkey. There was a close-up shot of Gramma and Madison making a pie together.

"Oh, wow! That's the first sweet potato pie she ever showed me how to make!" Madison said.

"See?" Mom said. "Everyone's still here. Our family isn't going *anywhere*, honey bear."

"I love you," Madison said.

"I love you more," Mom said, winking.

Madison sighed. She knew no family was perfect, but she couldn't help but think that *her* family came about as close as a person could get.

It was perfect for *her*. That's what mattered most.

Mad Chat Words:

3:]	Doggy
:-#-	My lips are sealed
>:-<	I am angrier than angry
<:>==	Turkey
woof	Woof (what did you think?)
LMK	Let me know
WAI	What an idiot!
E2EG	Ear-to-ear grin
DTRT	Do the right thing
NBD	No big deal
IYSS	If you say so
BFN	Bye for now

Madison's Computer Tip:

The Internet can be so helpful with school projects. I search the Web for information on subjects like my Thanksgiving presentation with Egg. The only problem with getting information online, however, is that I need to make sure my facts come from the right places. **Double-check any information you might get online, because not all Web sites have accurate facts.** I usually go to Web sites like museums, libraries, or other big organizations when I look up information for school reports.

Visit Madison at www.madisonfinn.com

Take a sneak peek at the new

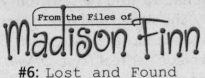

#6: Lost and Found

Chapter 1

No matter how hard she shoved, Madison couldn't squeeze all her stuff into the teeny green gym locker. She had hated gym class from the moment seventh grade started. The worst part was wearing the dreaded gym uniform. Its ugly blue polyester gym shorts made Madison's legs scratchy, and a too tight, white T-shirt with a blue Far Hills Junior High logo was not exactly the most flattering fashion statement. And wearing that shirt meant wearing a bra, even though Madison didn't have much to fill it out.

Even *WORSE* than wearing a scary, see-through T-shirt was facing the fact that Hart Jones would see her looking that way. Hart, Madison's big crush at school, just happened to be in her same gym section. He would see her wearing the ugly outfit!

1

Madison had to stop herself from over-thinking immediately. She sighed and took a seat on the small benches between locker banks. *Hart Jones*. Just the idea of him made her feel faint. Or was that because the locker room smelled like wet rubber floor mats and soccer balls?

She pulled her sweater over her head and wriggled into her T-shirt. Then she carefully yanked off her stockings and tugged on the polyester shorts under her wool skirt. They felt snugger than snug, and her legs prickled with goose bumps from the chilly air.

The locker area wasn't very full, so no one had seen her change. That was a major relief. Madison was standing alone in her row. Madison's homeroom had been dismissed early. Sometimes homeroom teachers let certain groups out earlier than others. However, neither of her best friends, Aimee or Fiona, had arrived from her homeroom yet.

Madison heard whispering in the next locker bank but didn't think much of it at first. Then she heard someone say *her* name.

"I can't believe I still have Madison Finn as my partner," the person grumbled with a huff.

Madison knew the voice. It was Poison Ivy Daly, her mortal enemy.

Ivy was speaking about their science lab. Their teacher, Mr. Danehy, had assigned Madison and Ivy as lab partners. He obviously didn't know how much they didn't get along.

"Just ignore her," Ivy's friend Rose advised. "What's the big deal?"

Madison stood on top of the bench, leaning into the lockers to hear whatever more she could hear. Ivy was there talking to her drones, Rose Thorn and Phony Joanie. Madison knew they might say not-so-nice stuff, but she still wanted to hear it. Unfortunately, the juicy eavesdropping stopped there. Madison's name wasn't mentioned again. They'd moved on to talk about hair. Ivy always wore her perfect red hair in perfect red clips.

As Madison stepped off the bench, the room got very quiet. Madison was surprised to see someone standing in the space between the locker banks. It was Ivy. And she was staring right at Madison.

"Hello, Madison," Ivy said curtly. "I didn't know you were in here."

"Yeah, well," Madison mumbled. She turned back to the green locker.

Madison wondered if, even for a fleeting second, Ivy felt a smidge guilty about gossiping without knowing who was nearby. But clearly Ivy felt nothing of the sort. She just *stared*. Madison felt Ivy's eyes watching her.

Rose and Joanie appeared from around the corner, too.

"Nice shorts," Joanie snapped to Madison. She was always snappy.

3

Madison felt her entire body shrink when Joanie said the words, however. *Nice shorts.* Ivy, Rose, and Joanie were wearing their shorts baggy and longer. They made the uniform look good. But Madison stood there in gym shorts one size too small.

"Excuse me!" Aimee Gillespie said, appearing from nowhere and sliding past the others into Madison's locker bank. Best friends have a way of showing up at just the right time. "Hey, Maddie!" she chirped.

Ivy raised one eyebrow at Aimee's entrance and walked away to find a mirror. Her drones followed.

"What was that about?" Aimee asked Madison.

Madison sat down on the bench again. Her shorts felt tighter than ever now. "These." She pointed to them.

"Huh?" Aimee shrugged. "Not everyone got the new shorts, I don't think. It doesn't really matter, does—"

"*New* shorts?" Madison asked incredulously. "*What* new shorts?"

Aimee explained that a letter had been mailed home with an order form for a new style of gym short. The administration had received complaints about the sizes being too small for a lot of girls. They were offering a new style.

"I never knew—" Madison said. Mom must have thrown out the mail without reading it. She did that sometimes.

"But you look great in those shorts," Aimee said. "You have nice legs."

"Thanks," Madison said. Maybe the shorts weren't so bad after all.

Fiona appeared with a flounce and a smile. "Helloooooo! Did you guys have a good weekend?"

She'd already changed into her gym uniform, pulling off her clothes to reveal the shorts underneath her pants. Fiona said it was easier to change that way. Of course she had on the loose shorts.

"Where did you get those?" Madison asked her.

"I don't know," Fiona admitted, a little spaced out. She sneezed. "They're more comfy than the other ones."

Madison would have to ask Mom to order her a pair of those.

"GIRLS!" A booming voice echoed into the locker room. Coach Hammond blew her whistle for emphasis. "LET'S GO! LET'S GO! INTO THE GYM!"

She wasn't as mean as a drill sergeant, but Coach Hammond was strict about starting class on time, lining up in perfect rows, and playing fair.

Madison hid behind Aimee and Fiona as they shuffled into the main part of the gym. She was happier than happy to see other girls wearing the shorter shorts.

"OKAY!" Coach Hammond yelled. She yelled even when she was standing nose to nose with a student. "TODAY WE HAVE PHYSICAL FITNESS TEST-ING! HEADS UP!"

Aimee turned to Madison. "This stinks. It's Monday morning. Who tests your physical fitness on Monday?"

"Yeah." Fiona sniffled. Then she sneezed three times in a row.

Madison was sitting on the floor between her friends, pretending to listen and watch Coach Hammond. But her eyes were wandering over to Hart. He was looking hunky, lying on his side across from them, whispering to Chet Waters, his new best friend and Fiona's twin brother.

"UPSY DAISY, BOYS AND GIRLS," Coach Hammond commanded. "EVERYONE UP AND INTO NEAT ROWS, PLEASE. WE NEED TO TEST YOUR AGILITY AND SPEED."

Coach didn't call it a race against each other, but kids pretended like it was. Everyone in the first row was paired up with someone in the second row.

Boys mostly paired with boys, except for Fiona and Chet, who led off the rows. They wanted to race each other for the obvious reason.

Coach Hammond didn't hear their friendly exchange.

"Eat my dust," Chet whispered to his sister.

Fiona smirked. "You—ah-ah . . . *CHOO!*" she said, sneezing again. "You *wish.*"

Coach Hammond explained that the task was to run up and down the length of the gym three times, then weave through the orange cones at the side of the room and run three more times up and back in the gym.

"I'm tired just thinking about that," moaned Hart. He was standing right behind Madison.

"ON YOUR MARK, GET SET . . . GO!" Coach Hammond blew the whistle and Fiona and Chet took off for the other side of the gym.

Madison couldn't exactly remember what she had to do during past fitness tests in middle school, but they had certainly never been like this. Kids were cheering on other kids, like it was a sporting event.

"Go! Go! GO!"

As Fiona made the turn to come back toward the group the second time, she collapsed to the floor.

"Ahhhhh!" a bunch of girls, including Madison, screamed.

Coach Hammond shooed them away and helped Fiona to her feet.

Fiona rubbed her elbows, since they'd slammed to the floor. She started to cough. "I feel hot, Coach."

She was *burning* hot, as it turned out. So the feverish Fiona was sent to the nurse. She waved to Madison and Aimee as she left the gym.

"She'll be fine," Madison said, trying to reassure Aimee.

"LET'S GET BACK IN LINE, BOYS AND GIRLS," Coach Hammond ordered. Everyone obeyed. The paired-off test subjects started up again.

Years of ballerina twirls helped Aimee to pass the fitness test easily. She was fast *and* graceful. Her running companion was some girl Madison only knew a little. The girl had to stop halfway through the test to take a big puff from her inhaler. She was one of two asthmatics in the class, but she still passed the test.

Most kids passed. When their turns came, boys and girls sped up and down the gym without even breaking a sweat.

Madison always knew she was good at running, or at least she was good at running *away*. But right there in the heat of the moment, she was losing her nerve. She had a fear that she would be the one to *not* pass. She'd be the one who fell into a sweaty, lumpy pile.

She looked over to see who'd be racing by her side. It was Ivy, who made a face.

Madison leaned over to retie her sneaker. Out of the corner of her eye, she caught Hart looking her way, too. She thought he was smiling a little.

"Hey, Finnster," he called out.

Some kids giggled at the nickname.

Madison gulped.

"ON YOUR MARK, GET SET . . ."

As soon as Coach Hammond screeched, "GO," Madison was off and zipping across the gym. She didn't pay attention to how fast Ivy was going. She turned at the first wall and never looked back. Even when an orange cone got knocked over in the middle of the test, Madison ran on. She huffed and puffed as she finished up. . . .

"IT'S A TIE!" Coach Hammond wailed.

Madison looked over at Ivy as they walked over to the sidelines, expecting her to grimace or pout or make her poisonous sneer.

But Ivy *smiled* instead.

"That was wicked hard," Ivy said, breathing heavily. She walked away.

Madison shook her head and adjusted her short shorts to make them a teeny bit longer.

Seventh grade could be wicked hard.

"I hope Fiona's not really, really sick," Aimee whispered to Madison as they changed back into their school clothes in the locker room after gym ended. "Oh my God, what if she is really, really sick?"

"She isn't," Madison said, hoping that her friend was okay. She pulled on her stockings leg by leg. "Nurse Shim just probably called her Mom."

"Let's call her later," Aimee suggested.

Madison grabbed her things out of the teeny green gym locker and climbed the stairs up toward the computer center. Her math textbook felt heavier than heavy inside her bag. Madison had a giant exam coming up the next day; she had barely reviewed the first half of the chapter.

When Madison walked into Mrs. Wing's classroom, she found her favorite teacher seated at her desk. She was gazing out the window at the dark, blue-gray sky.

"Looks like stormy weather," Mrs. Wing said softly, her glass bead earrings jingling as she turned her head to face Madison. "Looks like snow."

Madison sat down at her desk. "Cool!"

Mrs. Wing chuckled. "I don't like this cold. Winter is my least-favorite season. Brrrr." She faked a dramatic shiver.

"Mrs. Wing, do I need to come after school today to help with the Web site?" Madison asked, changing the subject. She had signed on to help as an assistant school cybrarian, which meant inputting polls, answering questions, helping to keep the school data, and more. Lately extra-credit homework and volunteering at the Far Hills Animal Shelter took preference over the Web, but Madison wanted to start working on the computer more.

"I was speaking with Walter about helping with the data entry," Mrs. Wing said. "And Drew, too. There's always room for helpers."

Walter Diaz, otherwise known as Egg, was Madison's best guy friend. And Drew Maxwell was Egg's best friend and therefore Madison's friend, too, by association. Not only were the two boys into computers as much as (if not more than) Madison, but they had their own Web page development in progress. Madison wanted to build her own site one day, too.

"So what are we adding to the site?" Madison asked Mrs. Wing.

Mrs. Wing smiled. "I want to add a Winter Wonderland section with news about hockey games and winter festivals and everything else going on inside and outside the school."

"What's up, Maddie?" Egg called out as he strolled into the computer lab. "What are you doing here so early?"

The second-period bell rang and Drew walked into class along with everyone else. "Hey, Maddie," he said, sliding into a cubicle of his own and giving her a wave.

While Mrs. Wing got the rest of the class settled, Egg was talking nonstop about his brand new skates.

"I just got these killer hockey skates," he boasted. One of Egg's greatest goals in life was to play for the New York Rangers hockey team. "I can't wait to try them out. They're black with silver stripes on the side."

"Like racing stripes," Drew quipped. "You wearing them tomorrow?"

"What's tomorrow?" Madison asked.

Egg gasped like he'd just been punched. "Oh, man! You don't know about it? A whole bunch of kids are going down to the Lake Wannalotta after school tomorrow."

"Who set this up?" Madison asked.

"Me and Chet. Didn't we tell you?" Egg replied.

"No." Madison rolled her eyes. "Anyway, I don't see what the big deal is with skating."

"What planet are you from?" Egg asked. "Skating is *WAY* cool."

"My cousin used to be a hockey skating champion at his old middle school," Drew said. "That was definitely way cool."

"Your cousin?" Madison asked. "You mean Hart?"

Drew nodded.

"So . . . Is Hart going to be skating, then, too?" Madison asked.

"Of course, Maddie," Egg cracked. "Everyone is going. You can't miss it."

Madison looked down at her desk and sucked in her breath. She didn't know how to skate very well, a fact that never seemed to matter before, but now it mattered a lot. She chewed on the inside of her lip and thought about her options. Could she just skip the whole skating scene without attracting too much attention? And while she was at it . . . . wasn't there a way she could get out of her math test, too?

Egg leaned over and pinched her shoulder before returning to his seat. "You better be there," he said. "Or I'll never let you forget it."

Madison just nodded and smiled.

She'd figure out what to do later.

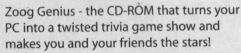
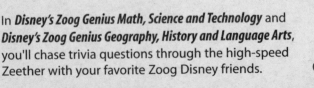